BENCHWARMERS

BENCHWARMERS

JOHN FEINSTEIN

FARRAR STRAUS GIROUX · NEW YORK

Farrar Straus Giroux Books for Young Readers
An imprint of Macmillan Publishing Group, LLC
120 Broadway, New York, NY 10271
Copyright © 2019 by John Feinstein
All rights reserved
Printed in the United States of America
Designed by Aimee Fleck
First edition, 2019

1   2   3   4   5   6   7   8   9   10

fiercereads.com

Library of Congress Cataloging-in-Publication Data

Names: Feinstein, John, author.
Title: Benchwarmers / John Feinstein.
Description: First edition. | New York : Farrar Straus Giroux, 2019. |
    Series: Benchwarmers ; [1] | Summary: Told in two voices, Jeff stands by his
    teammate, Andi, who fights to get on the sixth-grade soccer team and then must
    face opponents who target her for being a girl.
Identifiers: LCCN 2018056247 | ISBN 9780374312039 (hardcover)
Subjects: | CYAC: Soccer—Fiction. | Sex role—Fiction. | Sportsmanship—
    Fiction. | Middle schools—Fiction. | Schools—Fiction.
Classification: LCC PZ7.F3343 Ben 2019 | DDC [Fic]—dc23
LC record available at https://lccn.loc.gov/2018056247

Our books may be purchased in bulk for promotional, educational, or
business use. Please contact your local bookseller or the Macmillan Corporate
and Premium Sales Department at (800) 221-7945, ext. 5442, or by email at
MacmillanSpecialMarkets@macmillan.com.

To Jane Bluthe Feinstein—
who would make Andi proud—
and to the memory of Margot Pettijohn,
who made me proud

1

"MICHAELS, WHAT THE HECK ARE YOU DOING HERE?"

The mere sound of Ron Arlow's voice made Jeff Michaels cringe.

He had just pulled on a blue-and-gold gym shirt with MERION MUSTANGS emblazoned across the chest, and there was Arlow taunting him before he could even get out of the locker room. He took a deep breath and turned in the direction of Arlow's voice.

"The same thing as you, Arlow," he said, trying to sound as matter-of-fact as possible. "Trying out for the team."

Arlow smirked. He was at least five inches taller than Jeff, probably five foot six to Jeff's five foot one. Only a month ago, Jeff's parents had made a big deal out of Jeff going past five feet on his eleventh birthday.

Arlow was the jock king of the sixth grade at Merion Middle School. When teams got chosen in the schoolyard, he was invariably one of the captains. He wasn't the tallest kid in the class— actually Clara Daniels was—but he was clearly the most athletic.

Jeff had known Arlow since the third grade, when Arlow had enrolled at the town's elementary school. Back then, Arlow wasn't that much bigger than Jeff, but the first time they'd played touch football during recess, Jeff had lined up on defense against Arlow and then watched helplessly as the new kid raced past him to catch an easy touchdown pass as if Jeff were standing still.

It was the same in basketball: Arlow was the first kid in the class who could make a three-point shot. And in baseball, he was the best hitter Jeff had ever seen and made playing shortstop look easy.

Jeff wasn't bad at sports. He wasn't as strong or athletically gifted as Arlow, but he knew *how* to play. He wasn't the fastest player on any field or court, but he often anticipated where the ball was going and got there before the ball did. He never forced a shot in basketball—even though by the time he turned eleven he was a pretty good shooter—and knew how to find an open man.

Jeff had never formally joined a soccer team before, but he loved when his dad took him to see the Philadelphia Union, the city's Major League Soccer team, and he'd played enough pickup games at school and in the park near his house that he understood it and thought he had a chance to be pretty good at it—if only because of his ability to see things before they happened.

For as long as Jeff could remember, sports had played an important role in his life. His dad worked at NBC Sports–Philadelphia as a reporter, and Jeff often went with him to games and had met some of the area's most famous athletes, including Carson Wentz, the Eagles quarterback; Joel Embiid, the 76ers star center; and Jim Curtin, who had coached the Union.

He'd even met Rocky Balboa himself, when Sylvester Stallone came back to town for a dinner celebrating the fortieth anniversary of the most famous movie ever made in Philly.

The Hollywood star had been very nice when Jeff's dad introduced him, but all Jeff could remember about him was that he was not nearly as big a guy as he expected.

The sixth-grade soccer team was brand-new at Merion Middle—as well as at other schools in the region. Previously, sixth graders had been allowed to try out for the so-called varsity team—made up mostly of seventh and eighth graders—in each sport. Only on very rare occasions did a sixth grader make a varsity squad. Apparently enough parents had complained about their kids not having an opportunity to compete for an entire school year that Merion had created a sixth-grade boys' soccer team and a sixth-grade girls' field hockey team. There would also be sixth-grade boys' and girls' basketball in the winter and softball for boys and girls in the spring.

Jeff was thrilled when he first heard there would be sixth-grade teams.

This was day one of tryouts for the soccer team. Fifteen kids would make the team. Realistically,

Jeff figured his chances of making the cut were about fifty-fifty. There would be a basketball team in the winter. Jeff knew that would be his best chance to shine. His smarts and understanding of hoops would help him there. Soccer was more about speed and instincts. Jeff had average speed at best and wasn't yet certain if his instincts for the game were any good, since he'd never played it formally—and certainly never eleven-on-eleven on a real field. Four-on-four pickup was a long way from what he was hoping to do this fall.

Still, he had enjoyed playing pickup soccer even though he'd never actually joined a youth team. He had always played flag football in the fall and baseball, starting with T-ball, in the spring, so compared to some of the other kids who had played in youth leagues in the past, he was inexperienced.

Yet another reason why he was somewhat skeptical about his chances of making the team.

About the only thing he knew for certain was that Arlow would be one of the stars on the team. But he wasn't about to back down from his bullying.

As Jeff tried to walk past him to head from the locker room to the field, Arlow stepped in front of him.

"If you make the team," he said, "it'll only be because your old man's on TV."

Before Jeff could answer, another voice came from behind him.

"Shut up, Arlow," Danny Diskin said. "Give the bully act a rest. We'll all get judged by Mr. Johnston on how we play—nothing else."

Danny was about the same size as Arlow. He wasn't as good an athlete, but if a fight broke out, Jeff would probably bet on Diskin. Apparently, Arlow agreed. He waved a hand in disgust at Diskin and, rather than just move out of Jeff's way, turned and started jogging in the direction of the door.

"Thanks, Danny," Jeff said.

"I'd almost rather lose than play on the same team with him," Danny said. "Come on, let's go."

They joined the rest of the boys making the walk from the locker room to the field where the sixth-grade tryouts would be held.

Merion was a big middle school with about a thousand students in three grades. Its athletic facilities were sprawling: a main field with artificial turf, lights for night games, a running track, and grandstand seating for—Jeff guessed—a couple thousand people. Surrounding it were a patchwork of practice fields crawling with kids. The boys' and girls' varsity soccer teams, which had been practicing for two weeks, were already at work with their coaches.

Closer to the main redbrick school building was a worn-out field—more dirt than grass—that was mainly used for gym classes when the weather was warm enough. Now, it would be used by the sixth-grade soccer team.

As they walked to their field Jeff kept looking around, trying to count how many players were there and figure out where he might fit in terms of ability. He guessed there were about twenty-five guys.

"It'll be close," he said under his breath as they made their way to midfield, where two men waited.

Both were sixth-grade teachers. Hal Johnston, the head coach, taught geology in real life. Jason Crist, his assistant, taught American history. Jeff was in Mr. Crist's class and liked him a lot, even though the school year was only a couple of weeks old. He knew nothing about Mr. Johnston other than the fact that his friend Frank Rikleen—who was in his geology class—said he was very strict. Mr. Crist was strict enough, but he also had a sense of humor.

There was one other person waiting at midfield for them: Andi Carillo. She was in his history class and in his English class and was someone he rarely talked to—if only because he found her intimidating. She was a little taller than he was and had long dark hair that was now tied back in a tight ponytail. She was dressed like all the boys, in a Merion gym shirt and shorts. But unlike a lot of the guys, including Jeff, she also wore shin guards and cleats.

Mr. Johnston stood, arms folded, while everyone formed a circle around him and Mr. Crist.

"Okay, guys," he said. "A few quick things before we get started. You all know Mr. Crist, I'm sure. Out here we are *Coach* Johnston and *Coach* Crist. Or, if it's easier, Coach J and Coach C.

"We'll have three days of tryouts. Jason, how many signed up again?"

"Twenty-six," Jeff heard Mr. Crist—whoops, Coach C—basically confirm his earlier guess.

"Okay," Coach J said, nodding. "Fifteen will make the team, because that's how many uniforms we have and that's how many players we're allowed to have in uniform for each game. We'll play ten games against other middle schools from the north-central Philly area. The team that finishes first will get to play in the league championship game against a team from the south-central Philly area. So let's plan on eleven games, right?"

They all stared for a second, not understanding he was looking for a response. Then they got it.

"Right!" most yelled.

"That's 'Right, *Coach!*'" Coach J said. "Try it again."

They did.

"One more thing," he said. "I'm sure some of you know Andrea Carillo. She has opted to try out for our team rather than the girls' field hockey team. According to the school administration, she has the right to do this."

Andi—no one called her Andrea as far as Jeff knew, including the teachers in the classes he took with her—folded her arms and shook her head just a tiny bit as Coach J spoke.

"Does that mean I can try out for girls' field hockey?" Arlow yelled.

Jeff rolled his eyes. He glanced at Andi again, and now she was very clearly shaking her head in disgust.

"I don't know," Coach J said. "You might take that up with the powers that be if you want to, Arlow."

Jeff thought it was a great idea. Andi may have been intimidating, but from what he could tell, she seemed cool. He would much rather have Andi as a teammate than Arlow.

He was smiling at the thought when Coach J's voice brought him back to reality.

"Okay, let's line up for some stretching and calisthenics," he said. "Then we'll start to find out which sixth graders here at Merion know their way around a soccer field."

2

IT WAS HOT FOR MID-SEPTEMBER IN THE PHILADELPHIA area. Merion was located west of the city and was part of the string of the Main Line towns and suburbs known for being the location of Villanova University and many multimillion dollar homes.

By the time the coaches had put the candidates for their team through ninety minutes of drills, including shooting, dribbling, and passing, and vicious wind sprints called ladders, most of the boys were bending over, grabbing their shorts, and struggling for breath.

Andi Carillo was tired, too, but she wasn't going to let anybody—least of all the coaches—see her gasping or looking as if anything that had been asked had been too difficult.

She was keenly aware of Coach J's veiled shot at her when he had referenced her wanting to play soccer and that Principal Block had said she had "the right" to try out for the team.

Andi knew that Coach J didn't want her there. When she had brought in the consent form her parents had signed, he had looked at it, handed it back, and said, "Andrea, this is a boys' team. You can try out for field hockey. Or the girls' varsity soccer team next fall."

"I don't want to play field hockey, or wait a year to try out for varsity," Andi had said. "And I prefer to be called Andi. I'm a good soccer player. I know I can make your team."

"I'm sorry, it's nothing personal, but you can't make my team because it's a boys' team and you're not a boy."

He had stood up and handed her back the consent form. Andi's first instinct had been to throw the form back at him, but she resisted.

"If there's no girls' team in a sport, you have to give girls the chance to play," she'd said, not giving up just yet.

"Says who?" Coach J had said. "I set the rules for this team—not you."

Angrily, Andi had stormed out, feeling crushed. For weeks she had been fired up when she saw in the information packet sent to first-year students that there was to be a sixth-grade soccer team.

She had first played soccer with her two older brothers—who were now off at college—when she could barely walk, much less run. She'd played on her first youth team at six, and by the time she was nine, she was one of the top players on any team she played on. She was fast, could dribble the ball remarkably well for a kid her age, and had developed a strong, hard shot—even off her weak foot.

After the meeting with Coach J, she'd told her parents what had happened.

"Who does this guy think he is, Bill Belichick?" her dad had said, referencing the famous NFL coach. "He's coaching sixth graders!"

"Andi, you need to talk to the principal about this," her mother had said.

Andi had agreed.

* * *

The next morning, she had gotten to school early, marched to the office of Arthur L. Block, and asked for a meeting. His assistant had been puzzled why a sixth grader would want a meeting with the principal so early in the school year, but she told Andi to come back at lunchtime.

Andi had seen Mr. Block only once: at the opening assembly for the entire school on the first day of the school year. As she settled into the chair Mr. Block had waved her into when she'd come back for her meeting, she decided he looked the way a principal was supposed to look. He was tall, with short graying hair, horn-rimmed glasses, and a serious look on his face. Her impression was that he was a very serious person.

As soon as Andi started to explain what had happened, Mr. Block held up a hand, picked up his phone, and asked his assistant (Andi assumed) to find Mr. Johnston and have him come to the office right away.

The next five minutes were awkward: Mr. Block had asked Andi how she liked school so far and asked how her older brother Drew was doing in his first year at college. Andi had been relieved when Mr. Johnston walked in.

She had been less relieved when he began glaring at her as soon as Mr. Block told him what he thought about his meeting with Andi the day before.

"Mr. Johnston, this isn't anything new," he'd said, leaning forward in his chair. "At this age, girls can compete with boys. If we had a sixth-grade girls' soccer team it would be different. We don't. Andrea should be given the opportunity to try out."

"Does that mean you're going to let boys try out for the girls' field hockey team since there's no boys' field hockey team?" Coach J had said sarcastically. Andi wasn't 100 percent sure what a sneer was, but she'd suspected the twisted look on Coach J's face was one.

"I'll cross that bridge if I get to it," Mr. Block had responded, his tone very measured. "As far as I know, even at the high school and college levels there aren't very many boys' field hockey teams, so it *is* a little bit different.

"We created these sixth-grade teams to give the younger kids the chance to compete. If Miss Carillo wants the chance to compete with the boys, she's entitled to that chance."

"I still have final say on who makes the team?" Coach J had asked.

Mr. Block thought about that one for a moment. "As long as you give me your word you'll give Andi the same shot as the boys."

"I promise I'll be fair," he'd said.

Andi hadn't been even close to convinced. But there was nothing more for her to say at that moment.

By the time Coach J and Coach C gathered the team at the end of the third day of practice, there was no doubt in Andi's mind that she'd made the team. In fact, she was pretty certain she was one of the three or four best players on the field.

Even some of the boys who had appeared to not want her out there the first day had changed their tune. On several occasions when she went around players during scrimmages or scored, boys would call out, "Way to go, Andi," or "Nice play, Carillo."

Andi knew she had the best shot on the team. Others, notably Arlow, might have more power, but she was more accurate. Several of the boys didn't understand the offside rule and she spent some time explaining it to them.

She kept an unofficial count in her head of goals scored when they scrimmaged, and even though she spent most of her time playing midfield, only Arlow—who was never moved out of the striker position in front of the goal—scored more often than she did. A number of his goals came after she burst past midfielders and the defense had to come to stop her when she slid the ball to an open Arlow.

He never acknowledged one of her passes, but other boys did when she set them up.

The more often the others called her Carillo, the better Andi felt. Both Drew and Todd, her older brothers, would call her Carillo when she made a good play in the backyard. Everyone knew it was an unofficial jock way of saying, "You're good; you belong."

Andi knew she belonged.

"We'll post the roster tomorrow morning outside Mr. King's office," Coach J said. Mr. King was the school's athletic director—and an English teacher—and he had an office in the gym.

"Thank you all for participating," Coach J continued. "Coach C and I will have some hard decisions to make tonight."

As they turned to walk off the field, Andi noticed Jeff Michaels walking a half step behind her.

"Andi?" he said.

She turned and gave him a smile. He was shorter than she was, like most of the boys, but seemed nice in the classes they were both in. And, she had noticed the couple of times they had interacted, shy.

"Hey, Jeff," she said.

He pulled up next to her. He smiled—shyly. "I just wanted to say, because I don't know if I'll be around after today, that most of us not named Ron Arlow and maybe a couple of his dopey friends know you belong on this team. You're a terrific player."

Andi knew she deserved to be on the team—by a lot—but it was nice to hear it directly from one of the boys.

"Thanks," she said. "I think you should be on the team, too."

She wasn't completely sure if that was true. She hadn't really noticed how well he had played. He wasn't glaringly bad—or glaringly good. Now, though, she hoped he'd be on the team.

"I hope you're right," Jeff answered.

They had arrived at the entrance to the gym. Andi needed to go right, Jeff left.

"See you at practice Monday," she said, giving him a smile.

"That would be great," he said, blushing just a little.

They exchanged numbers before parting, and Andi turned toward the locker room feeling good. She had proven herself to a lot of the boys. She hoped that Coach J had noticed.

3

JEFF HAD TROUBLE SLEEPING THAT NIGHT. HE HONESTLY thought he'd played well enough during the three days of soccer tryouts to make the team—but he wasn't one of the coaches.

He knew he'd played better each day. He'd been a little bit intimidated the first afternoon, especially by some of the guys who clearly had real soccer-playing experience. But he'd gradually figured out that only a handful—one of them Andi Carillo—were clearly better than he was.

He was good at anticipating where the ball was going—much the same way he was good at it on a basketball court—and the drills the coaches had the players do at the start of each practice were helpful to him because he'd never done any in the past.

By the time the players scrimmaged for the final time on the third day, he felt a lot more confident with the ball on his foot and realized he had enough speed to stay with most of the others when he was defending.

He lay in bed, trying to run through the list of players he knew were better than he was, but his mind would wander and he'd have to go back and start over again. He finally drifted off to sleep convinced he was no worse than the tenth or eleventh best player on the team. Even if he was off by a couple, that should mean he'd be on the list in the morning.

When he got off the bus in front of the school the next day, he put on his favorite Philadelphia Eagles cap—the one commemorating their Super Bowl LII championship—and started walking through the halls to get to the gym at the back of the school. He was hoping not to run into a teacher who would demand he take off the cap indoors or, worse, someone who had already seen the list and would yell, "Hey, Michaels, you got cut."

Getting cut would be bad enough; hearing the news from someone else would be even worse.

He was relieved when he arrived at the bulletin board outside the gym office and found no one there. His bus was always one of the last to arrive at school—the closer a student lived to school, the later he or she was picked up—and that apparently meant that most kids had already checked the list.

The list was alphabetical. He started from the top: *Mark Adkins . . . Ron Arlow . . . Mike Craig . . . Danny Diskin . . . Max Friedman . . . Stevie Gillum . . . Allan Isidro . . . Taylor Jackson . . . Ethan Lewis . . . Jeff Michaels . . .*

He'd made it! He breathed a deep sigh of relief, then looked down and realized his hands were shaking.

Then a thought occurred to him. He went back to the top of the list and started again, and read all the way to the bottom—*Teddy O'Connell . . . Zack Roth . . . Terry Trang . . . Reed Whitlow . . . Bobby Woodward*—wondering if for some reason

Coach J had decided to list Andi underneath all the boys to make some kind of point. He hadn't. Jeff counted: fifteen names, none of them Carillo. That was impossible. In making his mental list the night before he'd had her as high as second—behind, sadly, Arlow—and no lower than fifth. She was definitely better than he was and, in fact, better than most of the boys whose names he was now looking at on the bulletin board.

He wondered what might have happened.

"Hey, Jeff!"

He turned and saw Andi walking up behind him. He could tell by the look on her face that she didn't know yet. She was smiling, clearly expecting good news.

"Did you make it?" she asked.

"Um . . . yeah, I did," he said. "Lucky, I guess."

Something in his tone must have warned her. The smile disappeared. She stepped around him and looked at the list. After a moment she put a finger on the printout and ran it down from top to bottom. Jeff could see anger in her eyes.

"It must be a mistake," Jeff said. "There's no way you didn't—"

He never finished the sentence because Andi had turned and was racing down the hallway. The bell was ringing, meaning kids had to be in their first-period classroom in five minutes or be marked late.

His joy at making the team suddenly felt hollow. He hoped it had just been a mistake.

As she ran down the hallway, Andi felt badly about leaving Jeff standing there with his mouth hanging open. It wasn't *his* fault she hadn't been on the list.

Like him, she wondered if maybe it was just a mistake—an oversight. Her gut told her that wasn't it. She wasn't sure what to do next. Go straight to Mr. Block's office? Call her parents?

No. She had to see the coach before she did anything else. Her heart pounding, she walked past the door to her first-period English class and went three doors down.

Andi followed several of Coach J's students into his classroom. The digital clock above the whiteboard said it was 8:28. The late bell would ring in two minutes.

Mr. Johnston was sitting at his notebook computer, writing something. While the other kids headed to their seats, Andi walked over to him. He looked up, saw her, and shut the computer lid.

"Ms. Carillo, did you take a wrong turn this morning?" he said.

"No, Coach, sir," she answered, trying to keep her voice from shaking. "I just checked the list for the soccer team and . . ."

"You're upset you didn't make the team."

That took the oversight option off Andi's list.

"Of course I am," she said, her voice rising. "You *know* I'm one of the best players—"

The late bell rang. Mr. Johnston stood.

"Ms. Carillo, if you come back here at the start of lunch period, I will gladly explain to you why you aren't on the team," he said. "For now, I'd advise you worry about getting to your first-period class with Mrs. Cohen, I believe."

He turned away from her.

"Good morning, everyone," he said to his students.

Andi stood frozen for a second, then turned and

walked briskly down the hall to her English class-room.

She walked in—a minute late—expecting Mrs. Cohen to say something. She didn't. Maybe it was because Andi had a look on her face that might burn a hole in someone.

4

BY THE TIME THE LUNCH BELL RANG, ANDI HAD DECIDED not to bother going back to see the coach. It was clear to her from his attitude that he felt good about cutting her, and it was unlikely—more like impossible, she figured—that anything she said was going to change his mind.

She hadn't wanted to involve her parents in the first place. She had known if Mr. Block ordered Coach Johnston to let her try out that he would resent it. It was now apparent that his resentment had led to her being cut.

Unfairly.

Which meant she had no choice. She wasn't going

to accept his decision without a fight. So instead of heading to the cafeteria to eat, she walked to the schoolyard, which was already crowded with kids digging into their brown-bag lunches and goofing around as they enjoyed the weather. After finding a quiet spot, she pulled her cell phone from her pocket and powered it on.

She knew her mother would probably be in a meeting of some kind but was counting on her answering when she saw Andi's number come up, since her daughter never called during the school day.

She was right. "Andi, I'm in a meeting," she said. "Is something wrong?"

"Yes," Andi said firmly.

"Can it wait five minutes?"

"Yes."

It took only three minutes for her mom to call back.

Andi told her what had happened and Coach J's response when she had gone to see him.

Her mother sighed. "Andi, I'm so sorry," she said. "Dad and I will help any way we can. What do you want to do next?"

Andi thought about it. She knew now she had been right not to go back to Coach Johnston. He wasn't going to change his mind, and she might lose her temper and say something she shouldn't.

Both her parents were lawyers. She wondered if there was something to be done legally.

"Can we take him to court?" she asked. "Make him put me on the team?"

Her mom sighed. "What you're talking about is getting some kind of an injunction right away," she said. "Those are usually used to get someone to stop doing something. I think it would be tough legally for a judge to order a coach to put someone on a team."

Sadly, that made sense to Andi.

"Let's talk about it when you get home," she said. "Dad's coming home from Boston this afternoon, right?"

"Plane should be landing about now."

That was good enough for Andi—for the moment.

She headed for the cafeteria, grabbed some chicken and a salad, and sat down by herself. She really didn't want to talk to anyone at that moment. She especially didn't want to talk to Ron Arlow, but there he was, walking in her direction and, uninvited, sitting down across from her.

"Got cut, huh?" he said, without bothering to say hello.

She kept her head down, as if the chicken was the most delicious meal she'd ever had.

"I don't know why you bothered in the first place," Arlow said. "The only reason you were even out there was that Block forced Coach J to let you try out. There was no way he was keeping a girl on the team."

The comment about Coach Johnston being forced to let her try out got Andi's attention. How did Arlow know that?

"Who told you that?" she said hotly, picking up her head to look at the smirking Arlow.

"Coach told my dad," he said. "My dad wanted to know what in the world you were doing out there, and so Coach J told him. He also told him not to worry because you weren't going to make the team."

Now Andi was really angry. It sounded like she'd never had a chance to make the team.

"I was good enough to be on the team and you know it," she said, glaring at Arlow.

"Not the point, is it?" Arlow said. "We don't need anyone on the team who bursts into tears the minute things get a little bit tough, do we?"

"You see me crying, Arlow?" she said. "You were the biggest whiner out there if anyone even touched you."

Arlow turned a little red, letting Andi know she'd hit some kind of nerve.

He was about to answer, finger pointed at Andi, when they heard a voice directly behind him.

"Give it a rest, Arlow."

It was Jeff Michaels.

"Why don't you go sit at that empty table over there with all your friends?" Jeff said.

Andi was the one smirking now. It might not have been an original line, but it was funny.

Arlow stood up. He was taller than Andi, which meant Jeff was giving up even more height to him. Not to mention weight and muscle.

"You want to be her knight in shining shin guards, Michaels? You want to take this outside? Is that what you want?"

Jeff put down his tray on the empty spot next to where Andi was sitting. Heads were turning in their direction at the sound of raised voices. The last thing Andi wanted was Jeff getting into a fight with Arlow on her behalf. For one thing, he would lose. For another, she didn't want a knight in shining armor of any kind.

"Let's go," Jeff said, just a tiny quaver in his voice. "I'm not afraid of you."

"Go where?" an adult voice said.

Walter Liggett, who taught eighth-grade English and looked old enough to have taught Benjamin Franklin's kids, was walking up to the table with a stern look on his always-stern face. Apparently he had cafeteria duty this week.

Both boys began staring at the floor.

"Nowhere, sir," Jeff said.

"Mr. Arlow?"

"Nowhere, sir," Arlow repeated.

"Good," Mr. Liggett said. "And just for the record, if I happen to hear about the two of you in a fight either during school, after school, or before school—and I will hear—you'll both be on detention until spring break. Understood?"

Both boys nodded.

"Understood?" Mr. Liggett repeated in a raised voice.

"Yes, sir," they both said.

Mr. Liggett turned and left. The two boys glared at each other for a moment, then Arlow picked up his tray.

"Watch yourself at practice, Michaels," he said. Then, looking down at Andi, he added, "No need to give you that warning, huh, Carillo?"

He walked away.

Andi was tempted to chase him down. Maybe he'd go outside with *her*.

Bad idea, she realized. Liggett was still lingering.

Jeff slid his tray across the table and said, "Mind if I join you?"

"Not at all," she said.

The funny thing about it was that Jeff probably never would have had the guts to sit down with Andi if he hadn't heard Arlow picking on her.

He felt badly that she had to put up with the jerk but was, truth be told, delighted to have an excuse to sit with her.

"I'm really sorry," he said softly, while she picked

at her food, head down, still shaking a little bit with anger.

"You don't have anything to be sorry for at all," she said. "Thanks for trying to intervene."

Jeff smiled. "I was actually glad Mr. Liggett showed up. Arlow probably would have killed me."

Andi managed a smile. "Who'd have thought that Wally Liggett would save your life one day?" she said.

They both laughed.

"You know, I've been thinking about what happened this morning," Jeff said.

"You mean—"

"You being cut," he said. "It's obviously unfair and wrong, and I might be able to help."

Andi was puzzled.

Seeing the look on her face, he pushed on. "My dad works for Comcast—I mean NBC Sports–Philadelphia; they changed the name a while back. This is the kind of story that people will talk about, especially nowadays when girls playing on boys' teams has been going on for years. It's ridiculous and . . ."

She stopped him, putting a hand up.

"What if you and I go talk to Coach J together?" Jeff said.

"That's really cool of you to offer," she said. "But before anything else happens, I need to see what my parents think. My guess is that my dad's first idea will be to go back to Mr. Block. He was the one who got me into tryouts in the first place."

"That makes sense, I guess. I'll talk to my dad about it tonight, see if he has any ideas."

She knew who his dad worked for—she'd seen him often on TV and especially liked the fact that he didn't just cover the Eagles and Phillies but also covered the Union and high-school football and basketball.

She reached a fist across the table.

"It will work out," she said. "Thanks for wanting to help."

Jeff smiled, bumping her fist with his own and trying to think of something clever to say.

Finally he settled for "You're welcome."

5

HAL JOHNSTON WASN'T SURPRISED WHEN ANDI CARILLO didn't show up to talk to him at lunchtime. He waited in his classroom an extra ten minutes to make sure she wasn't coming before heading to the faculty lounge, where almost everyone on the staff ate lunch.

He guessed that, just as she had done before, Carillo would go to Block, to complain about being cut from the team.

He smiled at the thought. He had anticipated that move and had gone to see the principal early that morning to tell him that he had decided to cut the girl and why.

"She's definitely one of the best fifteen players who tried out," he had explained. "In fact, based purely on her skills, she'd start as one of the forwards. But I have to put together the best possible team, and I think the presence of a girl will be divisive. It will be especially tough for boys not as good as she is to handle."

He'd thought this through. He didn't really have anything against the kid. But he simply didn't believe in coed sports teams. Boys should compete against boys; girls against girls.

If that made him old-fashioned, so be it.

Johnston figured Block probably wasn't yet forty, which made him at least ten years younger than the coach.

Which might have been why he wasn't surprised when Block had furrowed his brow before answering.

"Mr. Johnston, we're almost two decades into the twenty-first century," he said. "Boys playing on the same team with girls is nothing new. If she deserves to be on the team, she deserves to be on the team. Period."

Johnston had been expecting him to say that.

"Mr. Block, when I agreed to let her try out it was on the promise, from you, that I have final say as coach as to which fifteen players would give us the best team. This gives us the best team, regardless of talent level."

Block had laughed—which annoyed Johnston.

"Hal," he said, leaning forward, surprising him by using his first name. "We're talking about sixth-grade soccer, not the World Cup."

That comment annoyed Johnston. "Are we keeping score in these games? Is one team going to win and the other going to lose?"

"Sixth-grade soccer," Block repeated.

"You gave me your word I'd have final say."

For a moment the principal was silent. Then he said, "Yes, I did. Of course, I did so on the presumption that you would give the girl a fair shot to make the team. I'm guessing you had decided to cut her regardless of what you saw before the tryouts began."

"I cut her because I thought it was the right thing to do for the fifteen boys who made the team," Johnston said.

He remembered a famous line from one of the

Star Trek movies just in time to quote it to Block. "'The needs of the many outweigh the needs of the few . . . Or the one.'"

Block stood up. *"Wrath of Khan,"* he said, surprising his teacher. "A great line. I just don't think it fits here."

Johnston turned and walked out, not bothering to say anything more.

He assumed the Carillo family would protest in some form. Coach C had told him the girl's parents were lawyers. That could lead to some kind of legal move to force him to put her on the team. That was fine, too. A coach doing what was best for his team was hardly legal grounds to force him to change his roster.

If worst came to worst, he'd add her as a sixteenth player and let her sit on the bench. Not ideal, but if the boys understood she was there because a judge said she had to be, they might even be inspired to play better to stand up for the coach who had stood up for them.

"Win-win," he murmured to himself as he pushed open the door to the teachers' lounge. He couldn't stop smiling.

Andi's parents were waiting for her when she got home from school. Her mom had left work early to pick up her dad at the airport. Her dad looked pretty beat. He had been in Boston for the start of what would be a long trial involving one of his firm's corporate clients.

The three of them sat down at the kitchen table.

"Well, Andi, what do you want to do?" her dad said after getting some more details from his daughter. "Your mom and I talked, and we could go to court, but the odds are probably against us unless this coach admits you never had a chance to make the team because you're a girl."

"He basically said that to me," Andi said.

"Chances are he won't say it in court," her mom said. "I did a little research. The cases where judges have ordered that girls be given a chance have almost always involved being allowed to try out. You were allowed to try out."

"Even if I never had a chance," Andi said.

"The coach is no dummy," her dad said. "He let you try out, even if it was under his boss's orders, so in a legal sense he can claim you were given a fair chance."

"But I wasn't . . ."

Her dad held up a hand.

"Of course you weren't," he said. "And I'm sure everyone who watched the tryouts knows that. But in a legal sense it's much harder to prove. I would say our chances in court would be fifty-fifty—at best."

Andi felt pretty crushed.

She sat back in her chair, shaking her head in frustration. She looked at her mother, who clearly read her thoughts.

"Tony, there has to be some way to keep this from happening," her mom said. "Forget the legalities; this is about right and wrong, and what's happening here is just flat-out wrong."

"I know that, Jeannie," he said. "It's mind-blowing to me that this guy would do this to an eleven-year-old kid."

"I'll bet if they took a vote, most of the guys would want me on the team," Andi said. "By the end of tryouts there were only two or three of them still acting like jerks."

There was silence at the table for a moment. Her father finally stood up, went to the refrigerator, and took out a bottle of water.

"I honestly don't know what to do next," he said. "We can go to Block, I guess, but it doesn't sound like he's in a position to help at this point. We need a way to force people to pay attention to this."

Andi sat up in her chair, feeling the heaviness that had settled in her chest start to lift.

"Dad," she said, "that's it! We do know somebody who can do that."

She stood up and walked from the kitchen, pulling her phone from her pocket. She knew what to do next.

6

JEFF MICHAELS HADN'T REALLY ENJOYED HIS FIRST PRAC-
tice as a full-fledged member of the Merion sixth-
grade soccer team.

Coach J had given them a rah-rah speech before
practice started about how proud he was of all of
them for earning their spots on the team. He had
named Ron Arlow team captain without explana-
tion, since everyone knew it was because he was
the best player.

There was no mention of Andi Carillo—which
was no surprise to Jeff.

Practice began, and when it was time to scrimmage, the two coaches split the team into groups

of seven—with one player designated to substitute for both teams.

That player was Jeff.

The message was clear: In the minds of the coaches, he was the fifteenth player on a fifteen-man team. He could live with not being one of the starters once the games began, but he thought he was better than a number of the other guys.

Apparently the coaches disagreed.

When Jeff did get in, it took Arlow about thirty seconds to gather up a loose ball and charge directly at him. Arlow didn't make any move to go around him, just dribbled the ball right at him, as if to run him over.

Jeff froze. Suddenly Arlow faked left, then darted to his right and went around him as if he were a statue, Jeff diving at him much too late.

No one came to help him up. On the next whistle, he was back on the sideline.

Things went better on his second chance to get on the field. Danny Diskin broke down the middle and slid a pass to him. Jeff trapped it with the outside of his left foot and looked up to see Reed Whitlow charging at him. This time he didn't panic: He waited until Whitlow was almost on top of him, then feinted left and pushed the ball right with the inside of his foot, faking out Whitlow and racing past him to pick up the ball.

It was, Jeff thought, a pretty nifty move, and a couple of guys said so.

He held his own during his few moments on the field after that, even getting in briefly with Arlow's team and setting him up for one of the forty-three goals he scored during the practice.

Actually, it was more like five goals, but it felt like forty-three to Jeff.

After practice, Coach J reminded them that their first game would be the following Tuesday at home against Ben Franklin Academy, a private school and not a league game. They would get their uniforms on Monday and were told they needed to go out and get proper soccer cleats over the weekend. Some players already had soccer shoes. Jeff had been wearing sneakers.

"No spikes," Coach C warned. "They aren't legal in this league."

Jeff had showered and dressed and was walking out of the locker room when he checked the cell phone his parents had finally allowed him to have at the start of the school year. He'd spent most of fifth grade begging for a phone because all his classmates already had one. Okay, some of his classmates already had one.

His heart skipped a beat when he saw a text message from a number he recognized right away: Andi Carillo's.

Can u meet me in cafeteria before school starts in AM?

He texted right back: *OK. 8:15?*

That would give them fifteen minutes before the bell.

Great. See u then. Thx.

He wondered what she wanted to talk about— the soccer team, no doubt—but why him?

When he got home, he turned on the television. On NBC Sports–Philly, *SportsNite* had just started and the host was introducing a feature story he knew his father had been working on for a while about Saint Joseph's basketball coach Phil Martelli—who was getting ready to start his twenty-fifth season as the Hawks' coach.

Martelli was one of the more colorful characters

in college basketball, a guy who would say almost anything and get away with it because he was such a good coach.

"What do you like most about being a coach?" his dad asked Martelli on camera.

"Winning," Martelli said without hesitation. Jeff started to roll his eyes, but then Martelli continued. "And the thing I like second most is losing. It's all about competing, about being in that arena for forty minutes. All I've ever asked my players for is the chance to compete. If they give me that, I'm happy—regardless of the outcome."

Jeff thought that was a great answer, especially from such a successful coach. It was all Jeff wanted when it came to playing for Coach J and Coach C. He'd earned it but wasn't sure he was really going to get it. And all Andi wanted was the same thing. She'd earned it and was now being denied it.

He looked back at the screen, where his dad and Martelli were walking across the Saint Joseph's basketball court, talking to each other about why Martelli loved basketball in Philadelphia so much.

Martelli was talking again as his dad's story began to wrap up. "I can honestly say I've never worried about what the media thinks of the job I'm doing or what the fans think about the job I'm doing," he said. "Maybe that's why I get along with the media so well. I never take it personally when they criticize me. All I want is for my players to think I'm doing a good job and to look in the mirror at night and believe I've done the best job I can possibly do—every single day."

The shot of Martelli dissolved to one of him cutting down and waving a net in victory with a big smile on his face.

"Fair to say," he heard his father say in a voice-over, "that Martelli's been happy looking in the mirror for a long time."

Then Martelli's voice was heard again as his players swarmed to hug him on camera. "I love the winning," he said. "But it's the competition that I crave."

His dad came back on camera one last time. "The season starts November sixth," he said. "Phil Martelli can't wait. Tom Michaels for NBC Sports–Philadelphia."

Jeff didn't hear a word the host said when she came back on camera. Andi Carillo deserved the same chance as Phil Martelli, he thought. Maybe his dad could help.

Andi was waiting for Jeff when he walked into the cafeteria a few minutes early the next morning. The massive room was empty except for a couple of the kitchen staff who worked there, beginning their preparations for lunch hour.

If the presence of two students bothered them, they didn't show it.

Andi was sitting in one of the comfortable swivel chairs that the teachers used when they were monitoring the room. There were three of them. Jeff sat down next to her.

"Thanks for coming," she said. "This won't take long, one way or the other."

"No problem," he said. "Anything new?"

He didn't have to say "on the soccer team," because she understood.

"Not really," she said. "My dad and mom and I talked about maybe going to court to get an injunction, but they think that's a fifty-fifty shot at best."

"What's an injunction?" Jeff asked, baffled.

"It's when you say that someone is doing something that isn't allowed under the law and the court orders them to stop. In this case, a judge would have to say that, by law, Johnston can't keep me off the team."

"Can they do that?"

Andi shrugged. "In theory, I guess. If we can prove keeping me off the team is sexual discrimination, then the court could order him to put me on the team. It'd be the same if he tried to keep Danny or Reed off the team because they're black, or Max because he's Jewish."

Jeff understood. "But how do you prove that?" he asked.

"That's the problem," she said. "If he says he just did it because he thought his team would be better without me, that he gave me the chance to try out and I wasn't good enough, then they can't say he broke the law."

"But, clearly, you were good enough."

"Proving that might be hard. Even if every boy on the team said it, that wouldn't necessarily prove it. And, as you know, not everyone would say it."

"Arlow and his buddies," Jeff said.

"I have an idea, though," she said.

"I have one, too," he said.

She put up a hand.

"Hang on, let me finish. Do you think your dad might be willing or able to do a story on this on *SportsNite*?"

Jeff grinned. "I thought you'd never ask," he said.

7

THE FIVE-MINUTE BELL RANG JUST AS ANDI AND JEFF WERE wrapping up.

Jeff told Andi that he would speak to his father when he got home from school. Since it was a Friday, his dad would be covering a high school football game that night and would almost certainly be home during the day.

Andi wondered if his dad might be able to do something before the opening game on Tuesday. Jeff had no idea. He didn't even know if his dad would be able to do a story at all.

"Things have changed there in the last year or so," Jeff explained. "Before, Dad's bosses let him do pretty much any story he wanted to and this was the kind of story he liked doing. Now, though, everything is focused on the Eagles, Phillies, Sixers, and Flyers. He did a story on Phil Martelli last night, and he told me he had to fight to get them to let him do *that*."

"Why?" Andi asked.

"The way Dad tells it, they're more concerned with people clicking on their website than anything else. The Eagles get the most clicks—by far. Then the other pro teams. Then high school football—which he actually still enjoys. After all of that, college basketball. Maybe."

Jeff had asked his dad earlier that summer why he didn't do more stories about the Philadelphia Union. He liked reading online stories about the players, who came from different countries and backgrounds, but never saw much beyond a score and a highlight or two when he turned on his dad's station.

"The world's most popular sport is still a niche sport here in the city," his father had explained. "That means there's a small group of people who *love* soccer in this town. But they can't begin to compete with the other pro teams for clicks."

Jeff promised to report back to Andi as soon

as he had talked to his dad. There was no soccer practice that afternoon because the team would be playing games on the next several Fridays and Coach J had decided to give the team the day off to get an early start on the weekend.

Jeff had actually been a little disappointed. He felt as though he had made progress in practice and wanted the chance to show the coaches he deserved some playing time once the games began. He knew he wasn't going to start on Tuesday, but he was hoping to get into the game for more than the five minutes every player was required to play under league rules.

Catching up on some homework in the library at lunch, Jeff texted his dad to see if there was any way he could pick him up at school instead of having him ride the bus. His mom, he knew, was at work.

Anything wrong? his dad texted back.

No. Just would like to see you.

Usual spot @ 2:45.

Jeff's dad was waiting for him around the corner

from the front entrance to the school when Jeff walked out. This was their designated spot when either of his parents came to pick him up.

"Okay, so what do you want to talk to me about?" his dad said as Jeff tossed his backpack into the back seat and slid into the front.

"How did you know?" Jeff said as his father pulled away from the curb.

His dad smiled. Jeff had inherited his curly dark hair and, according to his mother, his smile.

"You enjoy riding the bus most days," his dad said. "You like hanging out with your friends— especially on a Friday. So if you ask me to come pick you up, something must be on your mind."

There were times when Jeff forgot that his parents were both pretty smart.

"Yeah, well, there is something," he said.

"Fire away," his dad said.

"There's this girl, Dad, named Andi Carillo," he started.

He saw his father grinning and could almost see his eyes brighten—even though he was wearing sunglasses.

"No, it's not that," Jeff said quickly. "I mean,

she's pretty amazing, but that's not why I wanted to talk to you."

"Okay then, what is it?" his dad asked.

Jeff began at the beginning and told him the whole story, finishing just as they turned into the driveway with Andi being left off the team.

It was a warm, humid mid-September afternoon, and they paused while his father checked the sky for any sign of rain before walking into the house. Once inside, they headed straight for the kitchen. His dad pulled two Cokes from the refrigerator and handed one to Jeff. They sat down across from each other at the kitchen island.

Jeff had explained as they got out of the car that Andi's lawyer parents thought her chances of getting some kind of court order to let her play weren't great.

"They're probably right about the court order," his dad said, sipping his soda. "So let me guess. You want me to do a story on this—embarrass the coach."

Jeff took a long sip of his drink, put it down, and nodded. "It's not fair, Dad, and he shouldn't get away with it . . ."

His dad put up a hand to stop him.

"I don't disagree, son. I just don't honestly know if I can get my bosses to invest my time and their resources into a story about sixth-grade soccer."

"The click thing."

His dad nodded. "Yes, the click thing."

Jeff had been prepared for that answer. "Isn't this story what you used to call a 'talkie'?" he asked.

His dad almost spit up his soda. "Where did you hear that?" he asked.

"From you," Jeff said. "You were actually talking to Mom about it one night in the car. You were talking about your early days working for the *Daily News*. You said a 'talkie' was a story that everyone would be talking about over coffee the next morning."

"That was back in the days when people read the newspaper every morning," his dad said. "But you're not wrong. To be honest, I thought we were pretty much beyond coaches keeping girls off teams, especially at your age. Sounds to me like your coach has never heard of Mo'ne Davis, which is hard to believe."

Mo'ne Davis, the dynamo from South Philadelphia

who had pitched a shutout in the Little League World Series and made the cover of *Sports Illustrated*, was living proof that girls could not just compete with boys, they could *beat* boys.

"Andi may not be Mo'ne Davis, Dad, but she's very good," Jeff said.

His father nodded. "Let me see what I can do," he said. "We need a plan."

8

ANDI WAS DOZING OFF WATCHING A BASEBALL GAME BE-
tween the Phillies and Reds when her cell phone
pinged to let her know she had a text.

She picked up her phone and saw that it was
from Jeff.

Call me, was all it said.

She was about to dial his number when she was
pinged again.

Please.

She smiled. She didn't know Jeff all that well,
but she knew he was polite to a fault.

She dialed.

"Thanks for calling right back," he said, which
made her smile all over again.

"What's up?" she said.

"What are you doing Sunday morning?"

The question was a bit odd, but she played along. "Not much," she said.

"Church?" he asked.

She laughed. "My parents tried it with my brothers and me until I was about eight. Then they figured out we were all going just for the doughnuts. So we haven't gone for a while. Why, what's going on Sunday morning?"

"I want you to go with my dad and me to the Eagles game," he said. "Sort of."

"Sort of?" she said.

"We'll get there early and go to the press box," he said. "Then we'll walk over to the TV studio and watch my dad do the pregame show. Then we'll go home."

"Why are we going to the stadium to not go to the game?" she asked.

She heard Jeff sigh on the other end of the phone.

"My dad wants to help," he said. "He thinks what Coach Johnston is doing to you is a story, but he knows his bosses won't go for it because it's not about the Eagles or the Phillies or the Sixers or the Flyers. They won't get it."

"So he's giving me a behind-the-scenes tour as a consolation prize?"

"Not at all. If he can get Michael Barkann and Ray Didinger to hear your story and get them on his side, he thinks he can get his bosses' attention. If he asks on his own, they'll just start saying, 'There's no digital traffic for a story like that, blah blah blah.' But if Barkann and Didinger back him up, they have to listen."

Andi knew who Barkann and Didinger were: Barkann was the longtime host of a weekday sports talk show and also hosted the Eagles pre- and post-game shows. Didinger was one of the most respected sports columnists in the city and also appeared with Barkann on the Eagles shows.

"So what does going to the game have to do with Barkann and Didinger?" she asked.

"They're going to meet us in the press box at ten thirty to talk about the story," Jeff said. "My dad thinks they should meet you. Actually he wants to meet you, too. He'll drive us to the studio, where he has to get ready to do the pregame show. We'll walk across the parking lot from there to the press gate. Then, after we meet with Barkann and Didinger, we'll walk back, watch the show, and then take Uber home."

"Why can't we stay for the game?" Andi was thinking if she was going to go to the stadium it would be fun to see the game.

"The NFL doesn't allow kids in the press box during the game," Jeff said. "We can go in there before the game but not during. That's why we're doing it this way."

Andi understood. "I'll ask my parents, but I think it'll be okay."

Once a year, Andi's dad took her to an Eagles game and they sat in his law firm's box—which was pretty cool. There was lots of food, and the seats were very comfortable. This would be different, she thought, but cool in a different way. Most important, it might help her get a chance to play soccer.

When she told her parents what Jeff and his father were proposing, her father smiled.

"I think the plan is fine—except why don't I see if we've got three seats in the firm's box. I can meet you there, you kids can watch the game, and then I'll drive you home.

"I gotta admit I'm a little jealous," he added. "I'd kind of like to meet Didinger and Barkann myself."

"Do you want me to ask if you can come to the press box?" Andi asked.

He shook his head. "No, you two kids should go on your own," he said. "It's a better story if it's two kids fighting to make a coach do the right thing. The less the parents are involved, the better."

As it turned out, Andi's dad was able to snag three tickets for the law firm's box.

"We got lucky," he said. "Weather's supposed to be good, so a lot of guys are stealing one last weekend at the beach."

That was fine with Andi. Even if Mr. Michaels couldn't do the story, she was getting a chance to see the press box at "the Linc," as everyone in Philly called Lincoln Financial Stadium, and see the Eagles play the Lions. In all it should be a pretty good day.

It was warm and sunny on Sunday morning when Jeff and his dad got in the car to drive to the stadium. The temperatures were supposed to hit the low eighties during the game, warm in Philly for mid-September, but not uncomfortable.

They picked Andi up at her house and pulled into the media parking lot shortly before ten fifteen. The guard didn't even look at Mr. Michaels's parking pass, just waved him in with a "Good morning, Tom," and a friendly salute.

NBC Sports–Philly was actually located inside the Wells Fargo Center, where the 76ers and Flyers played.

"Just cross the street right there," Jeff's dad said, pointing at the road that separated the arena from the football stadium. "If you have any problem with security, just ask for Mr. Moore. He's the boss, and I gave him a heads-up you were coming."

They were supposed to meet Didinger and Barkann at ten thirty. Jeff's dad's philosophy was always to be a few minutes early when possible.

"Especially," he said, "when the people you're meeting are doing you a favor by being there."

There were no issues with security. Their credentials clearly read, PREGAME ONLY, so if the guards had any doubts about letting a couple of eleven-year-olds into the press box, they were assuaged.

They went through security and took the elevator up to the press level on the sixth floor. Then they walked through the double doors leading to the press area and were struck by how crowded the room was even at 10:25 in the morning for a 1:00 p.m. kickoff.

Jeff stood and looked around the room. He was relieved when he saw Didinger walking in their direction with a cup of coffee in his hands.

"Jeff, good to see you again, buddy," he said, shaking hands. He turned to Andi and said, "I'm guessing you are the soon-to-be-famous-we-hope Andrea Carillo?"

"Andi," she said, accepting his hand.

"Come on, Andi," Didinger said. "Let's get you and your sidekick something to eat before Michael gets here. If we're lucky he'll only be a few minutes late."

Led by Didinger, they went through the buffet line—Jeff grabbing some French toast, Andi scrambled eggs. Didinger simply refilled his coffee.

"I eat at home in the morning on game days," he said. "Food's a lot better there. I stick to coffee here."

Jeff didn't see much wrong with the food but figured Didinger had eaten in about a million press rooms in his career.

They found an empty table near the back, and Didinger said, "Let me apologize in advance for Michael. He's the only guy I know who can show up late for a live TV show and get away with it."

"Not fair," a voice said behind them. Michael Barkann, also with coffee in hand, had walked up while Didinger was talking about him. "I'm never late for a live shot. Only taped ones."

He had a friendly smile on his face. Introductions were made. Everyone sat.

Barkann looked at Andi and said, "So, young lady, Jeff's dad tells me you're quite the soccer player."

9

AT THE URGING OF THE OTHERS, IT WAS ANDI WHO TOLD THE story. Occasionally Jeff jumped in with a detail—like an incident with a handful of the guys, led by Ron Arlow, who had attempted to bully her during a scrimmage—but she told most of the story herself.

Only at the end, when describing her brief meeting with Coach J after the team list had been posted, was there the tiniest quaver in her voice. Jeff noticed that the soda he was sipping from was shaking a little bit when Andi talked about the posting of the team list.

The two reporters looked at each other when she finished, as if deciding who should speak first.

It was Barkann.

"The truth is, a couple of years ago, we wouldn't even need to have this meeting," he said. "Tom would have just come in, talked to me, and we'd have assigned him a crew to go out to your school and do the story.

"This time of year, the Eagles are always most of our show, and we've only got a half hour nowadays."

"Used to be ninety minutes, just a few years ago," Didinger inserted.

"Right. And it used to be that no one calculated how many Web hits a story would get before deciding whether to do it," Barkann said. "A story was a story. Period. This is a story—period."

"Except . . ." Andi said.

"Except now we have to sell it to people who think a story is only worthwhile if they think it'll get those Web hits I mentioned," Barkann said. "It may be that we need to lure them into this, go through a back door."

"What do you mean by that?" Jeff asked.

"We start with Ray," Barkann said. "They never tell him what to write for the website because, well, he's Ray Didinger, and if you have someone writing for you who is in the Pro Football Hall of Fame, you don't mess with him."

"When he's writing about pro football," Didinger said. "Something like this might not be quite so automatic."

"Come on, Ray," Barkann said. "You write the Eagles for Monday, then write something midweek on Andi. Change of pace for the readers."

Didinger smiled. "I suppose I could do that," he said. "Maybe write it on Tuesday or Wednesday."

"But the first game is on Tuesday!" Andi said, then stopped herself, realizing she was raising her voice.

"I think we have to accept the fact that, realistically, you aren't going to play Tuesday," Barkann said. "Our goal is the long term."

"When's the next game?" Didinger asked.

"Friday," Andi and Jeff said at the same moment.

Barkann nodded. "Ray, if you can write the column for Tuesday, I'll bet we can generate some interest and get a crew out to the school with Tom on Wednesday. I'll push to get it aired that night."

"And if all goes well," Didinger said, "the

combination of the column and Tom's piece will put all sorts of pressure on the coach by the time he gets to school on Thursday morning."

Jeff looked at Andi. "What do you think? Sound like a plan?"

"How would you do it?" Andi asked.

Didinger looked at his watch. "I can spend some time right now interviewing both of you. I'll need some contact information for the coach and for the principal. I can call them tomorrow and have the column up early on Tuesday."

"Coach Johnston won't talk to you," Andi said.

"That's fine," Didinger said. "I just need to make the call so I can say I gave him a chance to tell his side. What about the principal?"

"I think he'll talk," Andi said. "He's a decent guy. He's the one who made Coach Johnston let me try out. He just didn't know the tryout was fake."

Didinger took out a digital recorder. "Everybody ready?" he said.

Everyone nodded. "Andi, I'll start with you," he said. "Michael, make yourself useful, okay? Get me some more coffee."

* * *

It didn't take long for Andi and Jeff to retell the story.

When Didinger was finished with Jeff, the two kids went back downstairs with Barkann and Didinger and across the street to the NBC Sports–Philly studio. Andi and Jeff watched most of the pregame show and then they headed to the suites' entrance back at the stadium with Andi's dad, who had met them at the studio during the broadcast.

The security line was short, because the game had just kicked off and most fans were already inside. They took the elevator up to the suites' level, and Jeff was not surprised to see another big spread of food lying just inside the door. They bypassed it to take their seats.

The Eagles were well on their way to winning the game 31–14 when Mr. Carillo suggested leaving to beat the traffic at the start of the fourth quarter. That was fine with Jeff. He was wiped out. It had been a fun day but a tiring one.

Ray Didinger had promised to keep everyone posted on whether he was able to reach Coach Johnston or Mr. Block the next day. Other than waiting to hear that news, there wasn't much left to do.

They were home in time for the postgame show,

and Jeff sat and watched his dad and his colleagues discuss the Eagles' chances to add to the Super Bowl they had won at the end of the 2017 season.

At lunchtime the next day, Jeff and Andi both got a text from Jeff's dad.

Just heard from Ray. He talked to Block. Helpful, he said. Nothing from Johnston so far. More later.

"Coach J won't talk to him," Andi said.

"Probably right," Jeff said. "But Mr. Didinger didn't think it mattered much."

Andi smiled. "I'll tell you when it will matter," she said.

"When?"

"This afternoon at practice. I'll bet you anything Johnston will figure your dad's behind this somehow and he'll blame you."

Jeff hadn't thought about that. He smiled, too. Then he laughed, remembering the words from one of his parents' favorite Billy Joel golden oldies.

"Only the good die young," he said.

* * *

It wasn't as funny when he got to practice. Coach J didn't say anything, but when the players lined up to stretch, Coach C came over and waved Jeff to come talk to him.

"What's up, Coach?" Jeff asked, surprised. He liked Coach C. He didn't appear to take himself nearly as seriously as the head coach did.

Coach C looked around for a moment as if he was about to do something he really didn't want to do.

"I'm guessing you know that Coach J got a call from Ray Didinger today," he said quietly, draping an arm around Jeff's shoulders and steering him away from the other players, who were no doubt wondering what was going on.

Jeff hadn't planned on this happening. For a moment, he was tempted to play dumb and say something like, "Ray who?"

But that clearly wasn't going to fly.

"I didn't know for sure that he'd call, but I guess I'm not surprised," he said.

Then, feeling a little braver than he probably should have, he added, "As long as Coach J believes he did the right thing by cutting Andi, there's no reason for him not to talk to Mr. Didinger."

Now it was Coach C's turn to look surprised.

"What I think Coach J wants to know is how Ray Didinger got involved in a story involving a sixth-grade soccer team."

Jeff shrugged. "He and my dad work together. I thought you knew that."

"So you told your dad about Andi being cut?" Coach C said, almost sounding accusing in his tone.

"Of course I did," Jeff said. "Andi's my friend, and my dad is, well, my dad."

Coach C nodded.

"Well, my advice for right now is to say nothing to Coach J unless he brings it up," he said. "He wanted to kick you off the team, but I think I've got him talked out of that. At least for now."

Jeff didn't say anything in response.

"Go finish stretching," Coach C said. "And try to stay out of Coach J's way the rest of practice."

Jeff jogged back to his teammates. Coach J, he was convinced, was glaring at him. Jeff looked the other way.

10

ONCE STRETCHING AND DRILL WORK WERE OVER, THE PLAY-
ers were again divided into two teams—with one
player watching from the sidelines. Jeff wasn't the
least bit surprised to find that player was him.

He got even fewer chances to see the field than
he had the previous week. The only reason he got
in at all, he suspected, was that Coach C would
wave him in to sub for someone when that player
looked winded.

He managed to make a couple of good plays on
defense, then made what he thought was a pretty
good nutmeg move with the ball, dribbling it in
between Taylor Jackson's legs and then going past
the defender to recover the ball and keep going.

He had open field in front of him when he heard a sharp whistle. He stopped and turned to see Coach J walking in his direction, hands on hips, whistle in his mouth.

"Michaels, if you want to showboat, you can go play in the schoolyard someplace," he said. "Or maybe show off your skills on TV. But on *my* team, you just play soccer. Understood?"

Arlow was constantly making what could be called showboat moves, and the coach had never called him on it. But Jeff wasn't Arlow.

"Understood," he said.

"Understood *what*?" Coach J roared.

It took Jeff a split second, then he got it. "Understood, *sir*," he said.

Coach J turned and walked away. "Blue team, bring it in," he said. Jeff—of course—was playing on the white team.

Then he blew his whistle again. "Diskin," he said to Danny Diskin, who was on the sideline at that moment. "Go for Michaels."

The thought of just walking off the field crossed Jeff's mind, but he decided against it: Why give the geology teacher an excuse to throw him off the team? If Coach J was going to do it anyway, fine, but Jeff wasn't going to make it easy for him.

At the end of practice, Coach J made them sprint the length of the field and back and then jog to midfield, where he and Coach C were waiting. Their field was not quite the full hundred-yard stretch of a regulation soccer pitch. But to Jeff, wind sprints made it feel twice as long after he'd been chasing down balls all afternoon.

That hadn't been a problem today.

"Okay, boys, good job out there," Coach J said. "We play here tomorrow at three thirty. That gives you forty-five minutes from the end of school to kickoff. Get to the locker room right away, change, and get out here, and we'll get you stretched out and warmed up."

He paused, and Jeff thought the day was mercifully over. It wasn't.

"One more thing, and listen up because this is important. For a lot of you this is your first experience with an organized team—emphasis on the word *team*. If you want to be part of a good team and also a good teammate, you remember always that you and your ego are no longer important. You do what's best for the team. You don't talk about team issues outside the locker room. What happens in the locker room or out here stays in the locker room and out here. Period."

He looked directly at Jeff. "Everyone understand?"

They all answered, "Yes, sir!" with Jeff barely moving his lips.

Coach J noticed.

"I said, do you understand—Michaels?"

"Yes, *sir*!" Jeff said in as loud a voice as he could muster.

"Okay then. Arlow, you're the team captain. Get everyone in for a cheer."

Arlow smirked, looked directly at Jeff, and moved to the middle of the huddle, his hand in the air. Everyone surrounded him.

"Team *first*!" Arlow said.

Everyone put their hands in and repeated, "Team *first*!"

They started toward the locker room, Jeff moving at a quick jog. The faster he got out of there, he figured, the better.

* * *

Ray Didinger's column was up on the NBC Sports–Philly website by the time Jeff got home.

His dad had texted him to tell him Didinger had finished writing it, so Jeff went straight to his computer to check it out.

Didinger pulled no punches.

"Andi Carillo is a talented eleven-year-old soccer player," it began.

> She's in the sixth grade at Merion Middle School and wants to play on the sixth-grade soccer team. But as of right now, she can't, because the team's coach, Hal Johnston, doesn't want any girls on his team.
>
> "No one ever said this was a boys-only team," Andi's father, Tony Carillo, said on Monday. "Presumably the best fifteen players—regardless of sex—would be selected for the team. That didn't happen."
>
> No one is disputing that Andi deserved a spot on the team based on her ability to play the game. What Johnston is apparently telling people is that he cut Andi because he thinks it would be bad for the morale of the boys on

the team to play with a girl who is better than they are.

I say "apparently," because Johnston didn't return a phone call, or an email as of this writing. It was left to the school's principal Arthur L. Block to defend his coach . . . sort of.

"Coach Johnston felt that boys should be on the soccer team and girls on the field hockey team," Block said. "I told him there was nothing in my mind that prevented Miss Carillo from trying out for the soccer team. He agreed to allow her to try out but insisted that, as coach, he should have final say on who made the team. I agreed to that."

I asked Block if he now thought that had been a mistake. There was a long pause. "Whether it was a mistake or not, I made a commitment to a coach who is being paid almost nothing to do a job that's important to the school," he finally said. "So I feel I need to stand by that decision and by the coach."

Block's heart appears to be in the right place. He doesn't want to break his word. But Johnston broke a commitment he made when he agreed to coach the team—spoken or unspoken. That was his commitment to give every kid a fair chance to make the team and to play for the team. Clearly he never intended to give Andi Carillo a fair chance.

The rest of the column had details about Andi and her family before it circled back to Didinger's conclusion.

The question of girls competing with boys dates to the 1970s. Girls have proven over and over again—Mo'ne Davis, anyone?—that they can compete with boys. It is heartbreaking in the year 2019 that there are still coaches who can justify this sort of segregation.

Next year will mark the one hundredth anniversary of women being given the right to vote. It would be nice if someone would wake Hal Johnston up to the fact that his way of thinking has been outdated for just about that long.

Jeff reread the whole thing again from beginning to end, then walked into the kitchen and told his mom to call it up on her computer. When she was finished, she smiled and said, "Well, that should get people's attention."

She was right. Jeff's dad walked in an hour later with a big smile on his face.

"Ray's column drew two-thirds as many hits in the first hour as the Eagles column he wrote last night," he said. "That's completely unheard of. Even the newsroom know-nothings couldn't ignore that."

"Are people talking about it? What are they saying?" Jeff asked eagerly.

His dad shrugged. "You know how the Internet can be. The comments section has some jerks, for sure. But seems like a lot of folks—most of the ones I'm seeing, at least—are really rooting for Andi and are outraged by the coach's attitude."

"So what now?" Jeff asked.

"Well, I will be at the game tomorrow with a crew. We'll interview Andi and her parents beforehand and see how Johnston chooses to handle himself after the game. If he tries to duck us, he's going to embarrass himself on camera."

"You think other media might show up?" Jeff's mom asked.

"Possible," his dad said. "Ray being the writer definitely gives it a lot more weight." He smiled. "Selfishly, I hope not. I'd like to have first crack at the story."

"Second crack," Jeff said.

"First TV crack," his dad said.

They both laughed. The next day would be interesting—regardless of the outcome of the game.

11

"DON'T BE NERVOUS, ANDI," TOM MICHAELS WAS SAYING. "We're taping this, so if you stumble or don't feel comfortable with a question, we'll just stop tape and start again. Remember, you're the good guy in this story."

Andi smiled and nodded her head.

She was standing in front of the camera that Mr. Michaels's cameraman had set up on a tripod. Behind her, about twenty-five yards away, the Merion–Ben Franklin soccer game was just beginning. She kind of wished Jeff was next to her to be her cheerleader, but he was sitting on the bench, in uniform, watching the game.

He had told her before the game that he expected to play exactly five minutes—the public-school rule in Montgomery County was that everyone in uniform had to play at least five minutes—and that would probably come late in the second half.

When the news team had arrived, as scheduled, at three fifteen, Mr. Michaels had told Andi and her mom that he had already interviewed the school principal.

"Principal Block said on camera that if he were the coach, you would be on the team," Mr. Michaels said. "That sets things up perfectly for us."

"Have you spoken with the coach?" Andi's mom asked.

Mr. Michaels shook his head. "I left him a couple of phone messages saying I'd like to talk to him after the game. Mr. Block gave me his cell number, and I texted him. We'll see what happens when the game's over. If he's smart, he'll talk. He can't hide forever. This story's making some waves in town."

He gestured with his left hand in the direction of another camera crew.

"I wish I was the only one here, but I'm not," he said. "The guys from Channel Three are here and

I think the *Inquirer*'s got someone out here, too. Plus, some internet sites."

"Would you prefer Andi not talk to anyone else?" Jeannie Carillo asked. "I mean, we owe you."

Mr. Michaels laughed. "Would I prefer you not talk to anyone else?—of course. But you need to talk to anyone who asks. The more people who are aware of this story, the better it is for your cause. Besides, we'll do a better job with it than anyone else anyway."

He turned to his camera guy. "John, you ready?"

The camera guy gave him a thumbs-up. "Count yourself in," he said.

"Ready, Andi?

"Ready," Andi said, though she wasn't really sure if that was the case when it came to being on TV.

"Okay then, three, two, one." He paused for a split second and then asked: "Andi, when tryouts ended for the team, were you confident that you'd earned a spot on the team?"

"Honestly I thought I'd made the team after the tryouts," she said, looking at the camera and not Mr. Michaels as instructed. "Several of the boys told me they thought I was one of the best players.

Plus, by the third day, a lot of them were being very encouraging whenever I made a good play. I thought that was a positive sign."

"So what was your reaction when you saw you weren't on the team?"

"At first I thought it was a mistake—so I went to see Coach Johnston. I knew he hadn't been thrilled about me trying out, but I thought I'd proven myself to him."

"And what did he say?"

"Well, I think to him, it didn't matter whether I was good or not—a girl on the team would be bad for morale."

"Do you think the boys on the team feel that way?"

She hesitated before answering that one. "Maybe a couple," she said. "But I think most would like to see me on the team."

Mr. Michaels smiled. "Perfect, Andi," he said. "You did great."

Andi noticed someone dressed like a reporter— shirt and tie, no jacket in the hot weather—talking to her mother. Then he walked up and shook hands with Mr. Michaels.

"Andi, this is Steve Bucci from Channel Three," Mr. Michaels said as Bucci walked over to shake her hand. "He'd like to ask you a few questions, too, if you're up for it."

Andi shrugged. Mr. Michaels had said it was okay with him, so it was okay with her.

"Sure," she said.

"Just give me a minute to get my crew set up," Bucci said. "I'm sure my questions will be pretty much the same as Tom's. Won't take long."

Andi nodded. Her mother came over with a towel.

"You're sweating," she said. "Let's sit in the shade for a moment so you can cool down."

Mr. Michaels was nodding. "That's a good idea," he said.

"What happens now?" her mom asked.

"We'll get some tape during the game, then see if we can talk to Coach Johnston and some of the players when the game's over."

"I'm sure Jeff will talk to you," Andi said, smiling.

"I'm sure you're right about that," Mr. Michaels said. "But interviewing my son is probably not the best idea. Don't worry, though. Even if nobody talks to us, I've got plenty for the story. And, like I said, with Steve and the other reporters being here, there's going to be a lot of pressure on the school to get this right."

Bucci was back. "Ready for your next close-up?" he asked with a friendly smile.

Andi's mother laughed.

"Give her one more minute to cool down," she said. "*Then* she'll be ready for a close-up or anything else."

Bucci hadn't been kidding about his questions being similar to Mr. Michaels's. He did ask a few more background questions, like "How much soccer have you played?" and "Did you learn to play from your two older brothers?" but the basic premise was pretty much the same.

After that, a newspaper reporter with a tape recorder and notebook asked if she had a few minutes. Her mom insisted they sit down on a bench in the shade of a large oak tree that wasn't that far from the entrances to the locker room.

More questions—all pretty much the same. The

reporter did ask if the family planned to go to court if Coach Johnston didn't relent and allow her to join the team.

"That would be up to my mom and dad," Andi said. "They're both lawyers."

"So no legal fees then?"

"I hope not," she said.

They heard some whooping coming from the direction of the Ben Franklin bench. Andi glanced at the scoreboard. The game was ten minutes old and Ben Franklin had just taken a 1–0 lead.

"Looks like Merion could use you," the reporter said.

"I sure hope so," Andi said, then stopped. She didn't want to sound like she was hoping the team would lose without her.

But she knew, deep down, that was exactly what she was hoping.

12

IF WATCHING HER SCHOOL LOSE WAS ANDI'S WISH, SHE got it. Ben Franklin led 3–0 at halftime before two goals by Ron Arlow midway through the second half—each half was thirty minutes long—cut the margin to 3–2.

But Ben Franklin scored with about eight minutes left to up the lead to 4–2, which was when Jeff Michaels got into the game. He was the last of Merion's fifteen players to see the field, and he actually played the last eight minutes—only because the game was a lost cause, he figured.

Ben Franklin scored once more in the final minute, and then it was over. The good news was this was a nonleague game. There were nine teams in Merion's conference, which meant there would be two nonleague games and then one game against each of the other eight teams in the conference.

Andi watched as the two teams lined up for hand-shakes. After the two coaches had shaken hands, Mr. Michaels appeared, as if by magic, at Coach J's side. Andi couldn't hear but could tell the conversa-tion was animated. At one point, Coach J pointed a finger at Mr. Michaels, who waved a disgusted hand in his direction and walked away.

"Hey, how'd it go with my dad?"

Andi looked up and saw that Jeff was standing right next to her.

"Good, I guess," she answered. "I just did what he told me to do—which was tell the truth." She ges-tured in the direction of Jeff's dad, who was now talking to Danny Diskin and waving his cameraman over. "Didn't look like it went so well with Coach."

Jeff shrugged. "He told us before the game that he wasn't going to be bullied into talking by, I think he said, 'some over-the-hill columnist,' and while he couldn't censor us, if he didn't like what we said, there might be consequences—like a lot of running at practice tomorrow."

"Danny doesn't seem too worried."

Jeff laughed. "Danny's not afraid of anything or anyone. Even Arlow won't mess around with him."

"You think anybody else will talk?"

"Arlow said he'd talk, but I doubt if he'll be taking our side . . . I mean, your side." He paused, cheeks a bit flushed. "You know what I mean."

"I do," she said. "I thought you played well today."

"How could you tell?" he said. "I only touched the ball a few times."

"And made a great tackle and a nice pass."

"You noticed?" he said. "Glad someone did."

She laughed. "I'm betting your dad noticed, too," she said.

"Yeah, probably," he said. "Unfortunately, he's not coaching the team."

"Unfortunately is right," she said, watching as Danny Diskin, interview over, walked away and Ron Arlow took his place in front of the camera.

Jeff texted Andi during dinner.

Dad says story will air tonight. Probably about 10:15. Then again in the morning, and tmrrw on 6 pm show. Lot of exposure.

Andi usually went to bed at about nine thirty on a school night, but there was no way she wasn't going to stay up to see Mr. Michaels's story. Steve Bucci had told her mom his story would air late, on the eleven o'clock news. She wouldn't stay up for that, but they would DVR it to watch in the morning.

Her parents were fine with the notion of her staying up a little late to watch the NBCSP report. The first fifteen minutes of the show seemed to take an hour. At least.

Finally, coming out of a commercial, anchor Dei Lynam set the piece up by saying: "It is the year 2019, more than forty years after girls first began playing Little League baseball. And yet, here in Philadelphia, there's at least one coach and one school that is still living in the past. Tom Michaels has more."

The piece opened with a shot of that day's game— showing one of Ben Franklin's goals.

Mr. Michaels's voice came from the television set as the Ben Franklin boys celebrated the goal: "Opening day for the sixth-grade soccer teams from Merion and Ben Franklin middle schools, and the visitors have just scored to wrap up a five–two victory over Merion."

The camera cut to a shot of Ron Arlow—which surprised Andi.

"First game, we're still getting used to one another," Arlow said. "We'll be better by Friday."

Then, suddenly, Andi was on camera, standing and watching the game with her mom.

"Experience may help Merion on Friday, but, unless Coach Hal Johnston backs away from his 'no girls on my team' edict, one of Merion's most talented players won't be in uniform—again."

The next shot was Andi talking about believing she had proven she had made the team during tryouts and that a number of the boys had clearly wanted her on the team.

As soon as she finished, Danny Diskin came on camera: "She was probably one of our three or four best players," he said. "If we had her playing up front, we'd be much tougher to stop. Today, we absolutely could have used her speed and touch with the ball."

The next shot was Principal Block. Mr. Michaels talked over him for a moment, identifying him and then letting him talk.

"It's a very uncomfortable situation," Block said. "I'm told Miss Carillo was clearly good enough to make the team, but I gave my word to Coach Johnston he'd have final say on who made the team. He believes, for morale reasons, having a girl on the team is the wrong thing to do."

The camera switched to Mr. Michaels sitting across from Mr. Block.

"You don't see that as a somewhat outdated approach?" Mr. Michaels said.

Mr. Block smiled sadly and shook his head. "I'd be hard-pressed to argue with you on that," he answered.

The next shot was of Mr. Michaels looking into the camera. "I tried to talk to Coach Johnston after today's game, but he was adamant in refusing to come on camera, saying he had nothing to say on the subject of"—he looked down at a notebook—"'girls trying to play on boys' teams.'

"He's right of course. Girls shouldn't play on boys' teams—unless they've earned a spot. Which is apparently the case with Andi Carillo here at Merion Middle School. Dei, back to you."

"Wow!" Andi's dad said. "That will stir things up. There's no way they can ignore that."

"And there's more to come," Andi's mom said.

Andi was texting Jeff. *Pls tell your dad THANKS*, she wrote.

His answer came right back. *Glad you liked it. We'll see what happens.*

He was right. The question now was what would come next.

13

AS LUCK—TRULY BAD LUCK—WOULD HAVE IT, THE FIRST
two people Jeff ran into when he walked into school
the next day were his teammates Ron Arlow and
Ron's best friend, Mark Adkins.

"Nice try, Michaels," Arlow sneered. "Your old
man's lame story isn't going to change a thing."

Jeff had watched the Steve Bucci piece on Channel Three before leaving for school, and it had hit
many of the same themes as his dad's story. He
had also read a column on the front page of that
morning's Philadelphia *Inquirer*'s sports section by
a columnist named Bob Ford. He'd then made the
mistake of diving into the comments section of the

columns online. Most sided with Andi, but a few were sickeningly sexist.

Since Jeff wasn't Ford's son, he'd seen no reason not to quote him.

"She's a much better player than I am," Jeff had told Ford. "She's a better player than most of us. To me, a coach's job is to have the best team possible. Leaving Andi off the team just because she's a girl makes us a weaker team."

He had a feeling Coach J wouldn't be too happy with that quote and he'd be in trouble—again—at practice that afternoon. He'd thought about that before talking to Ford. *What the heck*, he'd decided, *is he going to cut my playing time?*

Of course, Jeff might get thrown off the team. That was okay at this point. He'd proven something to himself by making the team, but he wasn't having a lot of fun, so if the coach wanted to be like that, fine.

All those thoughts flashed through his mind as Arlow stood in front of him, his face twisted into that ugly smirk.

"We'll see, won't we, Arlow?" Jeff said. "If I thought you could read, I'd tell you to check the *Inquirer* this morning. You might not be so confident then. My dad's not the only one on this story."

For a split second Jeff thought Arlow was going to hit him.

Arlow actually had his right hand balled into a fist. But, finally, he just shook his head and said, "You're not worth it," and turned and walked away.

Jeff breathed a sigh of relief.

When he climbed the steps to the second floor, which was where the sixth-grade classrooms were all located, he found Andi waiting for him at the top of the stairway. The five-minute bell was ringing when he saw her standing there with a huge grin on her face.

"I thought maybe you weren't showing up today," she said.

"I got . . . delayed," he said, deciding against repeating his conversation with Arlow.

"Well, guess what?" she said. "Mr. Block called the house this morning and asked if my parents can come in to meet with him and Coach J at lunchtime."

Jeff's eyes went wide. "You too?" he said.

She nodded. "Yup, me too. I don't want to get

carried away, but I think the plan may have worked. My mom says I have to stay off social media while this is going on, but she says that most people are just crushing Coach Johnston and the school."

"I'll bet that got Block's attention," Jeff said.

The late bell was ringing.

"I'll let you know," she said as they both started sprinting down the hall.

Thank goodness, Jeff thought, *neither of us takes geology.*

"I think everyone knows why we're here," Mr. Block said.

He had offered Andi's parents something to drink when they arrived, but they'd said, "No, thanks." Coach Johnston walked in a moment later along with Coach Crist.

Coach Crist introduced himself to Andi's parents before sitting down. Coach Johnston barely nodded at the three Carillos and Mr. Block as he sat down in the remaining empty chair.

"We're here," Coach Johnston said, "because it appears people can be intimidated by fake news."

Before Mr. Block could respond, Andi's dad jumped in.

"Oh, please, that tired claim doesn't work when the president uses it, and it certainly doesn't apply here. The stories said you cut Andi because she's a girl. What's fake about that basic fact?"

Coach J glared at Andi's dad, who glared right back.

Mr. Block intervened. "Hang on, gentlemen, let's keep this civil," he said. "There's no point in arguing tactics or fake news or anything else. Let's stick to what happens next. That's all that matters."

"Okay then," Andi's mom said. "What happens next, Mr. Block?"

Mr. Block sighed and looked at his head coach.

"The truth is I don't like feeling pressured into making decisions by the media or by social media for that matter," Mr. Block said. "But my gut has told me that the mistake here was mine, in telling Coach Johnston he could have final say on who made the team—regardless."

"That is what you committed to," Coach Johnston said. "And—"

Mr. Block held up a hand to stop him. "And if you

had made an unbiased and fair decision to keep Miss Carillo off the team, I'd have been fine with it," he said. "You didn't, though. You had no intention of putting her on the team, regardless of how she played. To me, now that the media has forced me to rethink, the deal we made wasn't adhered to in good faith."

"So you're going to overrule me and add Miss Carillo to the team," Coach J said.

"That's right. We will find her a uniform, and I'll pay for one out of my own pocket if need be. This may not be the right way to get to it, but I believe this is the right decision."

"You're just bowing to public pressure then," the coach added.

"Absolutely," Mr. Block said with a smile. "Because the public is right."

"Do you expect me to cut one of the boys to meet the fifteen-player limit?" Coach Johnston asked. "Jeff Michaels, for instance? Do you think that's fair?"

Mr. Block held up a hand. "I already spoke to the overseer for middle school athletics for the district. Not surprisingly, they are aware of the situation.

They are going to authorize all nine teams in our conference to add a sixteenth player—if the coaches so desire. By the way, apparently, other schools already have girls on their teams."

Coach J didn't have an answer for that. He stood up. "Well then, you should probably start thinking about finding another coach."

"I already have," Mr. Block answered. "That's why I asked Coach Crist to come to this meeting." He looked at his other teacher. "Jason, would you be willing to take over?"

Mr. Crist shot a glance at Mr. Johnston and sighed. Then he gave a rueful smile and said, "If necessary. And I'd love to have Andi on the team. It will make us better."

His fellow coach stood up and glared at him. Then he shook his head and walked to the door.

There was silence in the room, broken finally by Mr. Block.

"Hal, if you're at practice this afternoon, I'll assume that means you're going to continue as coach. If not, Jason, you're in charge—and your first job is to find Andi a uniform by Friday. Bill me if need be."

"Not a problem," Mr. Crist said.

Coach J, his face crimson, turned and walked out of the room.

"He won't quit," Coach C said after he was gone. "He loves coaching. And, deep down, he knows we'll be better with Andi on the team." He stood up and shook Andi's hand. "Welcome aboard, Andi. Can't wait to see you at practice today."

Andi stood up and accepted the handshake. "I can't wait, either," she said.

She meant it. But she was hoping that Coach C was wrong and that Coach J would be nowhere to be found at three thirty that afternoon.

14

JEFF GOT THE TEXT FROM ANDI AS HE WAS HEADING FROM his classroom to the locker room to get ready for practice.

I'm on the team! Coach J may quit! Here's hoping!

The hope didn't last long. Jogging onto the practice field, Jeff saw both coaches standing in their usual spot at midfield. For a split second he thought perhaps Coach J was going to tell the team he was quitting.

Andi was already there as the rest of the team assembled. Several of the other players tapped her on the back—clearly happy to see her. Others—notably Arlow and Adkins—refused to look at her.

"Gentlemen," Coach Johnston said—as if making a point. "As you can see, Miss Carillo has joined us today. Although I tried to make it clear to her that her not making the team wasn't personal in any way, she and her parents decided to take their story to the media. They succeeded in convincing Mr. Block that he should have final say on who is on this team. As you all saw during tryouts, Miss Carillo is a competent player and will be treated as such by me and by Coach C. I expect all of you to do the same."

"Okay, let's stretch," Coach C ordered.

Jeff was actually surprised that Coach J had been as gracious as he had been. Jeff had hoped Coach would quit, but this was probably as good as they could hope for under the circumstances.

When they finished stretching, Coach Johnston broke them into two teams of eight—taking three of his starting players, one of them winger Danny Diskin, and putting them with what was clearly the second team—which Jeff and Andi were both assigned to.

Shortly after the scrimmage began, Andi made a steal at midfield and quickly shot a pass to Diskin on the left side. She ran into an open space, and Diskin

slipped a neat pass to her, with only one player—
Mike Craig—between her and the goal. They were
playing without goalies—Bobby Woodward and his
backup, Allan Isidro, were doing diving drills with
Coach C—because the point of the scrimmage was
to work on their passing and shooting skills.

Andi faked as if to go to her right, then cut left
and slipped past Craig—who ended up sprawled on
the ground trying to recover from the fake. Since
she was a lefty, she transferred the ball smoothly
to her left side and kicked it high into the corner of
the goal. Even with a goalie that shot would have
been unstoppable.

Just as the ball hit the net, Arlow, peeling back
too late, slammed into her from behind and took
her down. Coach J's whistle blew, but Jeff barely
heard it. He was racing at Arlow, as was Diskin.

Diskin got there first, with Jeff and Stevie Gillum
close behind. Diskin slammed into Arlow and sent
him flying. Arlow was up in an instant, red-faced,
charging at Diskin.

He never got there. Coach C had seen the fra-
cas and raced in to grab Arlow, pinning his arms
and lifting him off the ground to stop him before

he could get to Diskin. Coach J ran in behind him, blowing his whistle repeatedly.

"*Everybody stop!*" he yelled.

Gillum was helping Andi up.

"You okay?" Coach J asked her.

"Fine," Andi said. "Fine." She was breathing hard, clearly a little shaken up, but there was no sign of blood or anything else wrong that Jeff could see.

"Who hit me?" she asked.

"Who do you think?" Jeff answered.

Coach J's face was dark with fury. "Let me remind you all of what I told you before we started today," he said. "We are a *team*. We do not knock our teammates down. In fact, Arlow and Diskin, those hits would probably get you ejected in a real game. Coach C, take these two and run them up and down the bleachers five times. Then send them to the showers."

"Coach, I think Diskin was standing up for his teammate," Coach C said. "I don't think this merits equal punishment."

Coach J put his hands on his hips for a moment as if deciding how to respond. "Well, Jason, when you're in charge, you can make those calls," he finally said. "Until then, please follow my instructions."

Coach Crist smiled—but it seemed like an angry smile. "You got it, Coach. Come on, boys."

Arlow turned to glare for a moment at Andi, who glared right back. Diskin walked over to her and pointedly gave her a high five, saying, "Sure you're okay?"

She nodded.

"Great play," he said loudly. "I hope everyone else noticed."

He jogged after Coach C, who had his arm around Arlow and was talking to him.

"Okay, seven-on-seven the rest of the day," Coach Johnston said. "Goalies, between the posts." Then he paused for a moment before adding, "Nice play, Carillo."

Ron Arlow was long gone by the time the rest of the team reached the locker room. Jeff was relieved. Diskin was still there, and Jeff asked him what had happened when they'd hit the showers after running the steps.

"Nothing, really," Diskin said. "Maybe he was just tired. I certainly was. He didn't say a word to me until he was almost dressed. Then he just said, 'You really think it's okay to have her on a boys' team?' I said, 'Only if she can play—and Andi can play.' He stared at me for a second, shook his head, and walked out."

Zack Roth, another of Arlow's cadre of friends, decided to stick up for his buddy.

"Ron just wants to win," he said. "Just like Coach wants to win. I heard the assistant varsity coaching job is going to be open next year and this season is Coach J's audition. He honestly thinks having a girl on the team will hurt morale, hurt our season. You saw what happened out there today."

"Yeah, we all did," Jeff said.

"Hey, she wants to play with the boys, she's gonna get knocked around," Roth said.

"Don't be such a tool," Mike Craig said. "That was a dirty play."

"This coming from the guy who got faked out of his shorts by the girl," said Terry Trang, another of Arlow's friends.

"Don't you see? That's the point," Jeff said. "She's

good. She can help us—if you guys will just let her play."

"Well, Michaels, I agree with you on one count," Roth said. "She can certainly help us more than you can."

"Yeah," Trang chimed in. "Maybe you can get your daddy to go on TV and say it's not fair you aren't playing."

Jeff took a step in Trang's direction, but Diskin cut him off.

"Easy, Michaels," he said. "One fight a day is enough for one team. Let's all just cool it and get out of here."

"Yeah," Craig added. "What is it those guys say in *The Three Musketeers?*"

The book had been on the summer reading list for incoming sixth graders.

"'All for one, one for all,'" Diskin said.

"That's it," Craig said. "Let's try that. At least let's try to try that."

Jeff was all for that idea. But he wasn't very confident it would happen in this locker room anytime soon.

15

ANDI WAS HAPPY WHEN PRACTICED ENDED. AND CONFUSED.

On the one hand the afternoon had gone almost exactly as she had expected—and feared. Coach Johnston had made it clear to the team that she was there only because Mr. Block had forced him to put her in uniform.

And Ron Arlow had—predictably—gone out of his way to cause trouble.

But there had also been noticeable support from a number of her teammates—not just Danny and Jeff, but from several other players as they walked from the field in the direction of the locker rooms.

Even Zack Roth, who she knew was pals with Arlow, had patted her on the shoulder while jogging by and said, "Good job out there."

And then there was Coach J's "Nice play, Carillo" after Arlow had knocked her down.

She reported all of this when her mom arrived to pick her up.

"I think most of the boys are going to figure out eventually that you can help them win," her mom said on the drive home. "Everyone wants to win, right?"

"I'm not so sure if Coach J or Arlow are willing to win with me on the team," Andi said.

Her mother smiled. "You said even the coach complimented you," she said. "I would say that's progress."

Andi couldn't argue with that. Any civil comment from him, much less a compliment, was progress.

She finished her homework quickly after dinner and decided to call Jeff to see if he could fill her in on what had happened in the boys' locker room after practice. Normally she had communicated with him away from school through brief texts, but now she just felt like talking.

He answered quickly—second ring. When she told him why she was calling, she heard him sigh. Then he filled her in on what he'd heard in the locker room after practice.

"Look, some guys are still clinging to the idea that a girl shouldn't be on a boys' team. The others were more like, 'If she can play, why not?'"

"Who said that?" she asked.

Jeff paused for a moment, thinking. "Well, Diskin you already know; Mike Craig—"

She cut him off. "Mike?" That surprised her, since it was Craig she had maneuvered past on the play that led to the goal.

"Yeah," Jeff said. "I guess he had the closest look at how good you are."

That cracked her up. It occurred to her that she couldn't remember the last time she'd had a good laugh.

The second—and final—nonleague game of Merion's season was against Isham Academy, a private school in Bryn Mawr, not far from Merion.

Coach Johnston had posted the starting lineup

in the boys' locker room, so Andi had to depend on Jeff to tell her that she wasn't starting—which didn't surprise her.

"Just remember, under the rules, he has to play you," Jeff said.

"Yeah, I know. Five minutes. Whoop-de-doo. You can bet that's all it will be."

Jeff smiled. "Might depend on how the game's going."

The game didn't go very well. Isham appeared to have a lot of experienced soccer players on their team. At one point during the first half Coach C wandered over and mentioned to Andi and Jeff and the other benchwarmers that almost the entire Isham team had played together in a youth soccer league. That explained why they clicked so well.

By halftime, it was 3–0. The break was only ten minutes, not enough time to go back to the locker room. The two teams sat on their benches and rested while their coaches talked to them. Andi stood—she'd been sitting long enough.

"Okay, we're going to bring Friedman, Jackson, and Lewis on to start the second half," Coach J said. "Mix things up a little bit.

"Craig, Trang, Adkins, you sit for a while, but be ready to go back in."

The three boys who were coming out of the game nodded. Andi knew that in pro soccer once you were out of a game you couldn't go back in. But at this level, players could return.

The lineup change meant that fourteen of Merion's players would have seen the field. The two exceptions were Andi and Jeff. No surprise there. Andi thought Jeff was every bit as good as—probably better than—the three players who were being subbed into the game. He was clearly in the doghouse because of his father's role in getting Andi on the team.

His crime was twofold: He was Andi's friend and his father's son.

Andi was different. She'd only done one thing wrong: been born a girl.

The lineup changes did little to affect the direction of the game. As Coach Johnston had said, Friedman, Jackson, and Lewis brought a different mix to the lineup—but it wasn't any better than what the three starters who were now on the bench brought to the game.

Mike Craig sat down on Andi's left—Jeff was to her right—as the half started.

"You should be in there," Mike said to her.

Andi looked at him. He was, in her opinion, the best-looking boy on the team. She had been aware of that even before tryouts started, since they were in two classes together. He had wavy blond hair and an easy smile. He wasn't smiling now.

"Thanks," she said.

Jeff jumped in. "This doesn't have anything to do with who the best players are, you know that, Mike," he said.

Craig nodded. "I know. And, for the record, Michaels, you should be playing, too."

It was hard not to like Mike Craig.

The score was 5–0 when Coach C walked over to where Andi and Jeff were sitting.

"Next whistle," he said, "you guys go in for Arlow and Roth."

Andi was surprised he was taking out two of his best players.

Coach C seemed to read her mind.

"We're going to put you in the striker position, Andi," he said. "See if you have any more luck than Arlow. Jeff, you're at midfield for Roth."

Coach C turned to Craig. "Mike, you're back in for Lewis."

That wasn't a huge surprise. Ethan Lewis's poor play on defense had been largely responsible for the two Isham second-half goals. He was a tall, gangly kid, probably better suited to basketball than soccer.

The three of them stood and walked to midfield so the coaches could signal for a sub on the whistle. Coach J didn't look at any of them.

The whistle blew.

Coach Crist signaled the referee that Merion wanted to sub. The Isham coaches were doing the same thing. Andi jogged in, Roth giving her a fist bump as they passed each other. Arlow looked her right in the eye as he went by but ignored her proffered fist.

There were about ten minutes left in the game, the outcome clearly decided.

About five minutes after the subs had occurred, Andi was looking over her shoulder at the sideline.

No one was standing as if to come in. Maybe they'd stay in till the final whistle.

Isham had a throw-in. Mike Craig ducked in and stole the ball. He weaved a few yards upfield and found Jeff open on the left side.

Unmarked, Jeff pushed the ball into Merion's offensive area. A defender came to meet him. Jeff saw him coming and sent a pass in Andi's direction as she was entering the penalty area. She gathered it in, faked to her left, then went right.

The goalie came out to try to cut the angle down on her shot. Out of the corner of her eye, Andi saw Teddy O'Connell on her right flank. She faked as if to slide the ball to her left foot in order to shoot and then slid the ball to O'Connell—who had a wide-open net because the goalie had come out to meet Andi.

O'Connell easily converted the pass, his kick hitting the back of the net. He turned and ran to Andi, pointing at her.

"Great pass, Andi!" he shouted, bear-hugging her the way soccer players do after a goal. Jeff came in from behind.

"You probably could have scored yourself," he said, also giving her a quick hug.

"Teddy was wide-open," she said. "I wasn't."

They turned to head upfield for Isham's kickoff. The game clock was now under four minutes. There wasn't time to rally, but at least they'd scored.

As she was lining up to prepare the restart, Andi heard a voice. It was Coach J.

"Ref, subs," he said.

Andi looked up and saw the four starters who had been on the bench—only Craig had gone back into the game—standing next to Coach J.

"Merion subs, come on out!" he yelled.

Puzzled—but not puzzled—she jogged to the sideline, Jeff right behind. Coach J said nothing about the goal.

Jeff went straight to Coach C. "Why are we out?" he asked. "We at least got the team on the score-board."

Coach J turned to him, giving him an angry look.

"That's a question for me, Michaels, isn't it?" he said. "You're out because I'm still trying to win the game."

16

THEY DIDN'T WIN THE GAME. IN FACT, ISHAM SCORED ONCE more in the final minute to make it even more humiliating.

When the players lined up for the postgame handshakes, Jeff fell into line right behind Andi. Several of the Isham players made a point of telling her what a great play she'd made on Merion's only goal.

"No idea why you aren't starting," said the Isham player who'd scored three of their goals.

After the handshakes and the exchange of cheers, Jeff looked up and saw a cluster of media members around Coach J. He'd almost forgotten that when he had told his dad on Wednesday that

Andi was on the team, his dad had done a short item on that night's broadcast about her change in fortune.

Clearly, a lot of the same people who had done the initial story had come back to follow up.

Jeff was surprised to see Coach J talking to the reporters. He knew the coach had refused to talk to his dad or anyone else for the initial stories. Now, he had about a half-dozen people around him, including a couple of guys with cameras.

Not his dad, though. He was in New York because the Phillies were beginning a crucial series with the Mets that night.

"We'll send a camera and an intern," his dad had said. "My guess is, if the coach talks, they'll use something from him, and if Andi does anything in the game they'll get something from her, too."

Rather than head for the locker room, Jeff lingered, inching closer to the circle where Coach J was talking. Both Andi and Danny had done the same.

"She'd had only one practice with the team, so I wasn't inclined to play her very much," Jeff heard Coach J saying.

"But why did you take her out after she set up

your only goal?" the NBC Sports–Philly intern said. Jeff knew who it was because she was holding a microphone with an NBC logo on it.

"She played ten minutes, and I had told the starters they'd get back in," Coach J said. "She made a nice play—but a lot of the credit for the goal should go to Mike Craig. He made the steal that set the play up."

"Six," the intern said.

"What?" Coach Johnston said.

"She played six minutes, not ten."

Coach J glared at her. Then he said, "Any more actual questions?"

Someone else asked how much playing time Andi might get the next time Merion played.

"We'll see how practice goes on Monday," the coach answered. "We're playing our first conference game Tuesday. I'm inclined to go with the guys who've proven themselves already."

Jeff almost gagged at that answer. Proven themselves? Those guys had been outscored 11–3 in two losses. No, 11–2, since Andi had been largely responsible for the one goal today.

Jeff felt a tap on his shoulder. It was Coach C.

"Locker room," he said, pointing in that direction. "You too, Diskin. Andi, you stay. I suspect these guys want to talk to you." He lowered his voice so Jeff, even standing a few feet away, could barely hear him. "Be careful what you say," he advised as the cameras and tape recorders began turning to find her.

Coach J was walking away, one guy with a notebook pursuing him. Jeff wanted to stay, but Coach C's message had been clear. He'd find out later what Andi said.

Andi wasn't all that eager to talk to the reporters, especially after Coach Crist's warning, but she knew she had to do it.

So when several of them asked if she could talk for a moment, she nodded her head and said yes. Coach C was still there, clearly to provide some sort of protection for her, and she was grateful.

"Give her some space, guys, back up a little," he said as one of the camera guys seemed to put his camera right in her face.

The same woman who had pointed out to

Coach J that Andi'd played only six minutes asked the first question.

"How do you feel about today?" she asked.

"It was great to be part of the team," Andi said—which was the truth. "I wish we'd done better," she added—also the truth.

"What about the way *you* played?" the same woman prompted.

"Well, I wasn't out there very long," Andi said, which brought a laugh. "But I thought I did okay."

Someone else asked the next question, a very tall woman, also with a TV microphone.

"Do you expect to play more in your next game?" she asked.

"I guess we'll find out Tuesday," Andi said. "I hope so."

She wasn't sure if that was careful enough.

"Okay, gang, thanks for coming out," Coach C said—a polite way of telling them that Andi was finished answering questions.

No one seemed to mind. The assistant coach put an arm around her and walked her away from the group.

"You did very well," he said softly. "Is someone here to pick you up?"

Andi's mom had been at the game but had been nowhere in sight—which concerned Andi. She looked around and saw her walking in their direction.

"There's my mom," she said, relieved.

Her mom walked up. "I'm so sorry, Andi, I just had to go to the ladies' room as soon as the game ended." She looked at Coach C. "Thanks for watching out for her."

"She did very well with the media," he said. Then he paused and added, "And in the game, too."

"Do you think she might start on Tuesday?" Andi's mom asked. "I mean, look what she did when she got a chance."

Coach C shrugged. "Not my call," he said. "But Coach J saw how well she played, too. We'll see."

He waved a friendly hand at both of them. "Gotta run," he said. "My son has a game at six."

"Your son?" Andi's mom said. "Where does he play?"

"Haverford High School," Coach C said. "And with Friday traffic, I'll be lucky to be there for the start."

He walked away. The field was now empty except for Andi and her mom.

"Seems like a nice guy," her mom said.

"I think he is," Andi said. "I just wish he was the coach."

Her mom nodded, watching as the coach broke into a jog. "I suspect if he was, you'd be starting on Tuesday."

Andi sighed. "Since he's not," she said, "I suspect I won't be."

17

HAL JOHNSTON THOUGHT THERE MIGHT BE STEAM COMING out of his ears by the time he got through talking to the reporters.

Jason Crist had pointed out to him that all the stories done about the Carillo controversy earlier in the week had made a point of saying he had "ducked" the media, or in the case of one guy on a radio talk show, had "cowered" rather than speak his mind. And the comments on social media were no better—every time a link went live, for every commenter that took his side, there were five more ripping his decision to shreds.

"Tell your side of it," Crist had told him.

"You don't even agree with my side of it," Johnston had shot back.

"Not the point," Crist had said. "I'm just telling you that the less you talk, the worse you look."

Hal knew he was right. That was why he'd agreed to talk after the game, even though the fact that Carillo had been responsible for the team's only goal was going to make things worse. Then he'd made the mistake of saying she'd played ten minutes, and that kid with the NBC Sports–Philly microphone had jumped on him.

He had turned his thoughts to getting into the car and listening to some music when he realized that someone was walking next to him. He looked to his left and saw a kid with a notebook and a tape recorder tagging along next to him.

"I'm done talking," he said, picking up his pace.

"That's fine," the kid responded. "But I'm Stevie Thomas, here for the *Washington Herald*. Up to you if you don't want to explain yourself."

Hal stopped for a second.

"Are you in high school or something?" the teacher said.

Thomas smiled at him. "Actually, I'm a freshman at Penn," he said.

"So why aren't you in class or the library?"

Thomas smiled again, the sort of condescending smile that made Hal want to say something he shouldn't. He decided to start walking again—he wasn't that far from the teacher parking lot.

"It's a Friday afternoon," the reporter said. "I do freelance work for the *Herald* when I have spare time. I pitched this to them after the initial stories came out earlier this week. They see you as a Last of the Mohicans."

"Excuse me?" Hal said. He got the reference, but he didn't like it.

"Girls playing with boys at this level has become a given," Thomas said. "From what I saw today, this kid is as good as anyone you have on your team. Yet you're still tilting at the girls-shouldn't-play-with-boys windmill."

Now he was mixing up the classics. "You wanna talk to me about a Spanish knight or a Mohican chief?" Hal asked, realizing he was smiling in spite of himself.

"Both," Thomas answered.

"Look, kid," Hal said. "I've made my position clear on this. I have nothing against the girl, and, you're right, she's a decent player—though not close to the best player on my team. It wasn't that long ago that you were eleven. How would you like it if you had to play a sport with a girl who was better than you? That'd be kind of tough, wouldn't it?"

Thomas shrugged. "My girlfriend was an Olympic swimmer," he said. "I was fine with it."

Now Hal was exasperated. "Did she swim against boys in the Olympics?"

"No, but she did when she was eleven at the local level and beat just about all of them. I suspect they were fine with it, too."

"Well, I'm not fine with it for the sake of these boys. My job is to do what's best for them—not what's best for the school principal because he doesn't want bad publicity."

Whoops, I've gone too far.

"That's off the record," he added.

Thomas laughed. "You want to go off the record, you say it *before* you make a comment."

Hal knew enough about the way journalism worked to know the kid was telling the truth. He'd made a mistake.

"Look, you're right," he said. "I apologize. If you

could leave out what I said about my boss, I'd be grateful. I'm kind of in a tough position here."

Thomas nodded. "I'm willing to do that," he said. "But in return, would you mind explaining to me the Don Quixote thing?"

Hal smiled. The kid was pretty sharp. Don Quixote was the hero of a hefty seventeenth-century novel that nobody read anymore. Quixote saw imaginary enemies as windmills and vowed to slay them all.

"It's not a sexist thing," he said. "I know it looks that way, but it's not." He had a sudden thought. "You a Star Trek fan?" he asked.

The kid gave him a look, then smiled. "'The needs of the many outweigh the needs of the few'?"

Hal nodded. "'Or the one.'"

"But are you sure that's what you're doing? If you had put Andi's being on the team to a vote of the boys, what do you think the outcome would have been?"

Hal thought about that for a moment.

"I think it would be close," he said. "There are boys who are adamant on both sides."

"Do you think if their coach was more positive

about having a girl on the team, the boys who are against it would be so negative about her?"

"Are you interviewing me or lecturing me?" Hal said.

Thomas seemed thrown—just a little—by that comment.

"Sorry," he said. "You're right. Bad habit of mine."

Hal had now reached his car. He chirped open the locks with his remote key. "Anything else?" he asked.

Thomas thought a minute. "Given the way Andi played today, will you think about giving her more playing time next week?"

"Sure," Hal said. "I'll think about it."

He got in his car and shut the door. He'd had enough questions for one day. He was glad he had the weekend to come up with some answers.

18

MONDAY'S PRACTICE BEGAN WITH A LECTURE FROM Coach J.

"We didn't play very well in either of our games last week, did we?" he said. Not looking for a response this time, he plowed on. "That's understandable because we were playing teams from private schools who have had sixth-grade teams for a while. That's why I scheduled those games before we began playing the games that matter—which start tomorrow when we go to Ardmore.

"They're like us, like all the teams in our league. This is their first year with a sixth-grade team. They only played one preconference game and they lost, just like we did. So this is our chance to get the season started in the right direction."

He paused for a moment to look at his players.

"Just so everyone understands, we're going to start the same eleven players we started on Friday. But Coach C and I have decided we're going to substitute earlier and more often. So the five of you who aren't starting, be ready. You'll be in the game in the first half."

Jeff looked at Andi, whose expression hadn't changed. This was a concession of some kind, but he wasn't sure exactly what it meant—except that they were going to get a chance before the last few minutes of the game.

As they grabbed mesh pinnies and broke into red and blue teams to scrimmage, Jeff saw Ron Arlow walking in his direction. This made sense because Jeff was dropping back to play defense, and Arlow was the striker for the starters.

"What are you smirking about?" Arlow said. "You think you've won because he's going to play your girlfriend more?"

"No one knows a smirk better than you, Arlow," Jeff said. "And if Andi—that's her name, by the way—helps us win, that means we've all won."

Arlow didn't respond, just turned his back to prepare for play to start.

The practice was rough, but it didn't get out of hand the way it had the previous week. The second team actually outscored the first—which made Coach Johnston's announcement that everyone would play the next day look very smart.

Jeff felt good about the day. The more he played—or practiced—the more confident he became, especially with the ball. And as a defender, he was getting better at reading the moves of an attacking player. At one point, Arlow came in on him one-on-one and when he tried to make a fake, Jeff stood his ground, took the ball off Arlow's foot, and started upfield with the ball.

He did glance over his shoulder to see if Arlow was going to try to knock him down from behind, but Arlow was just standing still, hands on hips. Jeff quickly passed the ball to Zack Roth, who sent a high looping pass to Andi. She controlled the ball with one touch, found Mike Craig open in the box, and he easily put it between the unguarded pylons.

It all really felt good.

When they were finished, everyone hot and

sweaty because it was still humid, Coach J was almost smiling.

"I liked the hustle today," he said. "Play like that tomorrow and we'll be okay."

He nodded at his colleague. "Coach C is going to give each of you a consent form that one of your parents or guardians has to sign." He went over departure and pickup times. "Any questions?" he asked.

Jeff had one. "Coach, will we need a different consent form for every road game, or is this one good for all of them?"

"Good question, Michaels," Coach J said—surprising him. "You'll need a different one for each road game. We'll have them for you at practice the day before each game."

Coach C handed out the consent forms, and they headed for the locker rooms. Jeff fell into step with Andi.

"Looks like somebody is rethinking things a little," he said.

She gave him her dazzling smile. "Maybe," she said. "Did you see the story online yesterday in the *Washington Herald?*"

Jeff had no reason to even think to look online

for anything in the *Washington Herald*. He shook his head.

"They ran a piece saying that Coach J admitted that he would think about reconsidering how much he let me play. Quoted him on it."

That, Jeff thought, would explain Coach J's comments today.

Andi stopped and looked at him. "Think about where I was a week ago—not even on the team. Then your dad did the story and others followed— including Stevie Thomas. Now I may get to really play tomorrow. It all started with *you*."

She gave him a quick hug, then turned and jogged in the direction of the girls' locker room.

Jeff stood there, staring after her. He had a feeling he had a stupid grin on his face, and he was vaguely aware of a couple of the other guys hooting at him.

"Way to go, lover boy," Danny Diskin said with a huge smile.

Jeff didn't care. All he knew was that Andi wasn't the only one who had come a long way in the last week.

* * *

It was raining Tuesday when they got on the bus—a steady, all-day kind of rain. There was no thunder or lightning, which meant they'd play the game unless the field was too soaking wet to play on.

The only player in uniform as the bus lurched toward Ardmore was Andi. Apparently there was no available girls' locker room near Ardmore's soccer field, so she had changed at school.

Jeff didn't really want to go outside in the steady rain, and the field was already looking pretty muddy as they stretched and warmed up. He was hoping the coaches might get together and decide to postpone the game.

No such luck.

It was too wet to sit on the bench when the game started, so the Merion benchwarmers all stood as close to the sideline as they could.

On the very first play of the game, one of Ardmore's players made a move on Danny Diskin, who slipped and fell into the mud. He came up absolutely drenched as the Ardmore player went in one-on-one against goalie Bobby Woodward and punched a shot past him. Woodward's unsuccessful dive at the ball left him just as muddy as Diskin.

Ardmore's 1–0 lead held up for a while after that.

It was tough to get traction going in any direction—the goal scorer's move being the exception—and the referee had to keep stopping the game to change to a new ball because the ones in play kept getting wet, heavy, and muddy.

Midway through the first half, Jeff heard Coach J yell the word he'd been dreading. "Subs!"

He was looking at all five of them. Coach C told them who they were going in for, and when the whistle blew they all jogged in.

It took Jeff about thirty seconds to find himself sprawling in the mud. The same kid who had made Diskin look so bad did the same thing to him. He faked left and went right. Jeff tried to plant his foot to go to his left and went down in a sliding heap.

Lying there, his first thought was that they were about to be down 2–0. But as the kid sprinted in the direction of the goal, he saw Andi flying back from her forward position. She caught up with the Ardmore kid—only later did Jeff find out his name was Evan Collins—and, with a brave slide, swiped the ball away from him just as he crossed into the penalty area. That allowed Woodward to run up and scoop the ball into his arms before the attacker could recover.

Jeff got to his feet and started to run toward Andi but she was already up.

"Way to save the day," Jeff hollered.

"No worries," she said. "Let's get going here."

He realized she was right. Soccer was a fluid game. There were no huddles between plays. Woodward had already kicked the ball in the direction of midfield, and Andi was sprinting in that direction.

Shut up and play, he told himself as the ball again skidded loose from players trying to get control of it.

It was still 1–0 at halftime. The rain had let up a little, but it didn't really matter, since everyone was soaked and the field was all but underwater. Not surprisingly, Coach J said the starters would all be back in to begin the second half but told the subs to "be ready at any moment."

Jeff had noticed that almost anytime the ball went near Andi, there had been two Ardmore players marking her. It occurred to him that if Coach J put her up front with Arlow instead of at midfield, it would be difficult for the defense to mark them both without extra help.

Almost as if reading his mind, Coach J called for Andi, Jeff, and Allan Isidro about five minutes into the half.

"Next whistle," he said. "Carillo, tell Roth to move back to midfield. You're up front."

Before the next whistle, though, Ardmore made it 2–0. Again, it was Collins. Fielding a deep pass from a midfielder, he dribbled around two defenders to the top of the penalty box and when Woodward came across to try to block his shot, he slid the ball to his left, to a wide-open teammate, who had a tap-in into the empty net.

Jeff saw Coach J's shoulders sag.

"Okay, guys, go on in," he said as he signaled the ref, and the three of them jogged onto the field.

"Come on, Andi, get us going," Jeff said as Andi took her spot next to Arlow. Roth had moved back to midfield wordlessly when Coach J had waved him in that direction.

Diskin sidled over to Jeff as play was about to resume. "Now," he muttered, "we've got our best team on the field."

"We'll see," Jeff said.

The clock had just ticked under thirteen minutes left in the game.

19

BRINGING ANDI ON DID TWO THINGS: IT STRENGTHENED
Merion's midfield, because Roth was better than
anyone else playing there, and gave the Mustangs
two legitimate scorers up front.

Still, it wasn't going to be easy to rally. With
a two-goal lead, Ardmore was playing conservatively, content to kick the ball deep whenever possible and force Merion to go the length of the field
to get into scoring position. Even then, there were
always at least six defenders back.

It was Jeff—much to his surprise—who started
the play that began to turn the game in Merion's
favor. He had noticed that Ardmore's midfielders
were content to kill time by moving the ball across

the center line, then turning and passing it back to one of their strong-legged defenders. He'd clear the ball deep in the direction of the Merion goal as soon as any Merion player ran toward him.

Jeff was playing defense but kept inching forward, since Ardmore wasn't really trying to score. He knew this was a gamble because if an Ardmore midfielder noticed him and passed the ball in Collins's direction, he'd be out of position.

Still, with fewer than eight minutes to play, there wasn't much to lose.

And so, when one of the Ardmore midfielders crossed into Merion territory and turned to pass the ball backward, Jeff was already on the move. Knowing he was way out of position, he darted between the midfielder and the defender and cleanly stole the ball. He had a running start and was past the stunned defender in an instant. Seeing him, both Andi—on his left—and Arlow—on his right—began running in the direction of the goal.

Jeff's quick move had put him beyond all but two of the Ardmore defenders. He kept dribbling the ball as quickly as he could, waiting to see which defender would come at him.

It was the one who was marking Andi. Jeff acted

for a split second like he was going to go right and pass to Arlow, then slipped the ball to Andi as she closed on the goal from the left. She was about to be one-on-one with the goalie when the other defender left Arlow and sprang at her.

Andi had drawn her left foot back to shoot, but when she saw the defender make his move, she regained control of the ball, dribbled it for one more instant and then, at the last possible second, slid it across to Arlow, who stopped it with his foot and in one quick motion booted it past the goalie into the upper-left-hand corner of the net. It was a goal worthy of ESPN's nightly top ten highlights. Or so Jeff thought.

Andi's ability to control the ball even as she was about to shoot was remarkable. Arlow's quickness in gathering and shooting was, too.

Arlow threw his arms in the air to celebrate and ran in the direction of the Merion bench yelling, "Come on now, let's win this thing!"

He didn't acknowledge Jeff or Andi. That was okay with Jeff. Andi ran at him and gave him a high five.

"Great steal—great pass!" she yelled.

"You too!" he said. "You put the ball right on Arlow's foot!"

They were both panting with excitement. Roth and Craig came up from behind.

"Hey," Roth said. "You guys just gave us a chance!"

"Tell Arlow that," Jeff said.

"I will," Roth said. "Later. For now, let's tie this thing up."

With just over a minute to go, they still trailed, 2–1.

Ardmore had changed tactics after Arlow's goal—smartly choosing to attack and keep Merion bottled up rather than make a mistake playing conservatively, the way they had earlier.

Unlike in professional soccer, where only the referee knows exactly how much time is left in the game because he is allowed to add seconds or minutes for injury time, everyone could see the scoreboard clock. There was no injury time. When the clock hit :00 the game would be over.

Ardmore had just hammered a long shot over Merion's goal, and Jeff could see the clock had just ticked under a minute.

With Ardmore's strikers back near midfield to cut off any attempt at a long kick from Woodward, Jeff was alone near his goalie, who rolled the ball to him and urgently screamed, "Go, Jeff, go!"

Fifty-five, fifty-four.

Jeff was unchallenged until he approached midfield. He looked to his right and saw Roth, who was the team's best ball handler. He slipped a pass to Roth, who came back to him to make sure no one from Ardmore would get in between them.

Roth took off down the right side, angling toward the sideline because Ardmore was bunching its players in the middle of the field, content to let Roth run wide and kill time.

Thirty-seven, thirty-six . . .

As Roth started to approach the goal area, Ardmore's defenders began to cut him off as he moved more to the inside for a better angle. With almost everyone in the middle of the field, Roth stopped suddenly and kicked the ball as hard as he could to the far left, where Andi came to meet the ball.

Arlow was cutting in the direction of the goal, his arm up, screaming, "Carillo, Carillo, here!" He had two players marking him and the goalie leaning in his direction.

Twenty-two, twenty-one . . .

Andi looked at Arlow and made a motion as if to kick the ball to him, then sent a no-look pass backward to Craig, who had moved up into the play with Jeff on his right.

Fifteen, fourteen . . .

The defenders tried to swarm Craig, but he coolly dribbled right as if trying to line up a shot or get the ball to Arlow and then knocked a quick pass back to Andi, who had now cut into the penalty area. Her defenders had leaned away from her for just an instant, thinking the ball was going to Arlow.

Six, five . . .

Craig's pass hit her in stride and, in one fluid motion, she slammed a shot to the goalie's right. He had been leaning left, thinking Craig would either shoot or try to find Arlow. He dived back, but it was too late.

The ball whooshed by him into the net.

Two, one . . .

The buzzer sounded, with the referee pointing at the net to indicate a goal had been scored. The Ardmore kids argued briefly that the goal had come after the buzzer, but it was useless—the goal was clearly good.

Everyone on the field in a blue-and-gold uniform charged at Andi.

"What a shot!" Jeff heard Roth say as a celebratory scrum formed around Andi.

"What a pass!" Andi said, pointing at Craig, who was leaning in for a giant hug.

The bench emptied, the five guys not playing coming to join the celebration. Arlow waited for the pandemonium to calm a little before he leaned in to Andi, patted her on the shoulder, and said, "Nice one, Carillo. Really nice."

Coach C had come to join the celebration and was giving everyone pats on the head. Jeff looked for Coach J. He was at midfield, shaking hands with the Ardmore coach.

Danny Diskin was looking in that direction, too.

"Wonder if he's happy," Jeff said.

"Well," Diskin said, "it was just a tie."

He was right—of course. But at that moment, it felt like a huge victory.

20

ANDI COULDN'T REMEMBER THE LAST TIME SHE'D FELT SO happy. Scoring the tying goal was great, but the reaction of her teammates was greater.

Even guys she knew hadn't wanted her on the team were mobbing her.

She knew it had to kill Ron Arlow that neither Roth nor Craig had opted to pass the ball to him in those final seconds. But, as the result proved, it had been the right play: She had space, and he didn't. What made her feel good was that they'd had the confidence to get the ball to her with the game on the line.

Andi also knew that Arlow would probably have

preferred to dive into the mud face-first than compliment her on the goal, but he had done it.

They went through the ritual handshakes with the other team, everyone covered in mud but hardly noticing at that point. When Andi reached Evan Collins, the Ardmore striker who had scored both their goals, he had a wide smile on his face.

"Good thing for us you didn't play the whole game," he said as they shook hands. He had wide brown eyes that lit up when he smiled, moppish—even when muddy—light brown hair, and an easy way about him that she didn't see too often in eleven-year-old boys. "You guys would probably have scored five if your coach knew what he was doing."

She smiled back at him. "Trust me," she said, "he knows what he's doing."

"Maybe he thinks so," Collins said, still smiling as he moved on to Jeff, who was next in line.

Others on the Ardmore team made a point of telling Andi how well she'd played. She cracked up when their goalie said to her, "That coach doesn't want you on the team, you can come and play for us."

It was clear that the stories about her battle to get on the team had been widespread—at least among those in the Philadelphia-area soccer community.

They did their cheers and headed in the direction of the locker room—except for Andi. Her parents had both been able to get away from their offices in time to see the end of the game, so she walked directly to where they were waiting near the entrance to the locker room.

Her father's eyes were shining when he hugged his mud-covered daughter.

"What a great goal!" he said. "That was spectacular!"

"Mike gave me a great pass," she said. "I think they all thought he'd pass to Arlow. That left me open."

"Andi, you aren't talking to the media," her mom said, laughing. "You're talking to us. You don't have to be modest."

"Okay," she finally said, "I'm the next Alex Morgan," naming her favorite star of the US Women's National Team.

"You never know," her dad said. "Someone's going to be the next Alex Morgan. Might as well be you." Then he turned serious. "What did the coaches say to you after the goal?"

"Coach C was out there celebrating with all the guys," she said.

"And his boss?"

"He said, 'Nice comeback, guys. See you at practice tomorrow.'"

"Figures," her dad said. "There are people in the world who have trouble admitting they're wrong. Let's see what happens Friday. If he doesn't start you after what happened today, maybe you have to think about talking to Jeff's dad again."

Andi shook her head. "No, Dad, I don't want to go through that again. I'd like to let my play do the talking."

Her dad smiled. "You sure you're only eleven years old?" he said.

She laughed. "You're the ones who said I'm eleven," she said.

Her mom nodded. "Trust me," she said. "You're eleven. I remember the night you were born vividly."

They turned and headed for the car. The rain had stopped, and Andi spotted a rainbow behind the school.

It didn't turn out to be quite as good a day for Jeff.

Like everyone else, he was pulling off his muddy uniform and getting ready to take a quick shower, when he realized someone was standing over him.

He looked up and saw Arlow. For a split second he thought Arlow was going to compliment him for starting the play that led to the first goal.

That turned out to be hopelessly wrong.

"You probably think you and your girlfriend are pretty hot stuff right now, don't you?" he said.

Jeff noticed several of Arlow's pals—Ethan Lewis, Mark Adkins, Teddy O'Connell—standing behind him, smirking. Zack Roth, supposedly an Arlow backer, had a towel wrapped around him and was heading to the shower.

"Arlow, what's your deal?" Jeff asked. "Without Andi, we would have lost that game. You know that."

"No, I don't. She made a pass to me that anyone else on the team—even you—could have made. And she was wide-open on the last goal because the defense was pulled over to my side. Craig and Roth made the play."

"That's nuts, Ron," a voice behind them said. "She made two killer plays."

It was Roth, who had apparently stopped on his way to the shower when he'd seen Arlow standing in front of Jeff.

Before Jeff could echo Roth, Danny Diskin pushed his way into the circle and jabbed a finger into Arlow's chest.

"What is your problem, Arlow? Do you just have something against girls? Is that it? Just admit it."

Arlow's response was to grab Diskin's arm and try to wrestle him to the ground. Other players were coming from all over the small room so fast Jeff couldn't tell who was trying to tackle whom. He was standing, trying to decide who he should go after when he heard an adult voice booming from the doorway.

"STOP! STOP NOW! ANYONE STILL FIGHT-ING IN FIVE SECONDS IS OFF THIS TEAM! FIVE. FOUR. THREE. TWO . . ."

Coach C stopped at two because everyone had scrambled free from whatever tangle they were in and stood. Several guys were grasping at towels to hold them up.

Coach C walked to the middle of the room, where he was surrounded by the fifteen boys in various degrees of dress and undress.

"I'm not even going to ask who started this or why," he said. "I'm pretty sure I know, but I really don't care right now. Fellas, we're a team. We don't fight one another; we fight the other guys. We work together to win. And that includes Andi Carillo!"

He was looking right at Arlow when he said that. Arlow looked right back at him.

Coach C shook his head. "Those of you going back to school, the bus is leaving in fifteen minutes, so if you want to take a shower you better get moving."

Jeff had seen his parents as he'd come off the field—his dad always had Tuesdays off during football season—so he didn't have to worry about the bus.

He was pulling his shirt on when he saw Arlow headed for the door, apparently to get on the bus.

"This isn't over, Michaels," he said in a menacing tone.

"Always have to have the last word, don't you, Arlow?" Jeff answered.

"And I will," Arlow said, proving Jeff's point as he walked out the door.

21

JEFF WONDERED WHAT PRACTICE WOULD BE LIKE THE NEXT day. He knew that—Arlow and his closest chums aside—everyone on the team now understood that they *needed* Andi playing to have a chance to be any good.

He also thought he had proven that he should be getting more playing time. At the very least it was encouraging that with the game on the line in the final few minutes Coach J had left both him and Andi on the field.

Andi called on Tuesday night. Apparently Danny Diskin had texted her to let her know what had happened in the locker room.

"Arlow just won't let it go, will he?" she said.

"He'll have to, sooner or later," Jeff said. "He's lost Craig and Roth. Even Coach J is giving in a little."

"Yeah, my mom is saying the same thing," she said. "But I'll bet I don't start on Friday. I'll bet you don't start, either—and you should."

"I'll bet you start," Jeff said. "When you've gotten the chance, you've been our best player."

"Arlow's still our best player," she said. "He might be our worst guy, but he's our best player."

"You create chances for other people," Jeff said. "Arlow only creates chances for Arlow."

She didn't answer that one. Jeff hadn't even thought about it until it came out of his mouth. She was better than Arlow because she made the others better. Arlow didn't do that.

Sadly, though, Andi was right about the lineup.

When they got to practice on Wednesday, Coach J's only message was that he was proud of them for not giving up when they were down 2–0, but they were going to have to play a lot better, "for the entire game, not just a few minutes," if they expected to have a chance to win any of their remaining seven games.

"We still haven't won a game," he reminded them.

"If we're going to change that beginning Friday, we have to play better from the first whistle."

When the coaches split them up for scrimmaging after ball-handling drills, the only lineup change was that Danny Diskin had again been moved from the first team to the second and that Reed Whitlow—who was a starter but played with the second team in practice—was at midfield with the starting unit.

"What do you think you did wrong?" Jeff murmured to Diskin as they lined up to begin play.

"I think I took Arlow on," Diskin murmured back. "Clearly a no-no."

Jeff certainly thought that was possible. But Coach J hadn't been in the locker room when the fight broke out, and Coach C hadn't been there when the fight started. Maybe Arlow had just reported back who the combatants were, not how it started.

They were all tired after playing in the rain the day before, so the coaches cut the practice a little bit short. It was a beautiful afternoon; the rain had cooled the temperatures and the sun was shining. Rather than have them all stand or kneel at midfield, Coach J asked everyone to take a seat on the bleachers. Whistles and shouts drifted over from the JV and varsity teams on the other practice fields.

When they were all seated, Coach J stood in front of them, hands on hips, and said nothing for a moment, as if deciding where to begin. Finally, he took his cap off, then put it back on.

"Look, everyone, Coach C told me what happened in the locker room yesterday," he said. "That's gotta stop for a lot of reasons. We all have to be on the same side. That's what team sports is about. We're a *team*."

He paused, then added: "I take some of the blame for this. A lot of the blame. I divided you guys because I made it clear I didn't think this team should be coed." He looked at his female player. "It was never personal, Andi."

Jeff was surprised. He'd never heard Coach J call *anyone* by their first name in practice or during a game. And, he'd never referred to her, at least as far as he knew, as Andi.

He went on. "You're a tough kid, and you're a good player. That doesn't mean I've changed my mind about whether a girl—any girl—belongs on a boys' team. The acrimony we've had in our locker room is proof of that."

Jeff wasn't sure exactly what *acrimony* meant, but he suspected it had something to do with people not getting along with one another.

"But you are on this team, and all of us—starting with me—need to let go of any notion that you're not part of the team."

He looked at Arlow. "You understand me, Ron?"

Arlow was clearly surprised and didn't answer right away.

"You understand me, Ron?" Coach J repeated, raising his voice.

"Yes, sir," Arlow answered.

"O'Connell?"

"Yes, sir."

"Adkins?"

"Got you, sir."

"Lewis?"

"Yes, sir. Got it."

Coach J didn't say anything to Roth or Craig, who had previously been in Arlow's camp but now had apparently accepted Andi.

"Okay then," Coach J said after Lewis's response. "I hope we're all on the same page now."

He paused again. "We'll have a short practice tomorrow before we play Main Line here on Friday. We'll start the same eleven that we did on Tuesday. See you tomorrow."

He turned and walked away. Jeff, sitting one row up from Diskin and Andi, leaned down and said, "What just happened? First he says he's sorry he didn't treat Andi like any member of the team, then he says he's not changing the lineup."

"Guess he's equal opportunity on an as-needed basis," Diskin said.

"As needed?" Andi said.

"Yeah, when we need a goal he's equal opportunity. Until then, business as usual. He'll put Andi and his other benchwarmers in only when we start losing."

Jeff stood up. "Well," he said, "that just means Andi and I will probably play early on Friday."

22

THE WEATHER ON FRIDAY WAS AGAIN PERFECT, AUTUMN having finally come to Philadelphia. The opponent was Main Line Middle School, and the crowd was pretty substantial. Good weather and a Friday afternoon were probably, Andi figured, the reason.

Then again, there had been an item in the *Inquirer* about her play on Tuesday, and on TV the previous night Michael Barkann had mentioned the fact that Andi "led Merion's rally to a two–two tie," during his coverage of prep action.

To Andi's amusement, Barkann reported an additional twist: A girl named Megan Tway had recently joined Main Line's team. She just hadn't received any attention because—apparently—no one had tried to keep her off the team. In fact, according to what Andi had heard, she was a starter on defense.

Not long after Merion had completed its stretching drills and the players had broken up into small groups to warm up, Andi saw someone in a black-and-white Main Line uniform trotting in her direction.

It was not a boy.

"Andi, I wanted to be sure to meet you," she said, putting out a hand. "I'm Megan. I've heard a lot about you."

Andi laughed. "Not for the reasons I'd like," she said.

Megan shook her head. "Actually, I've heard you're a really good player and your coach is making a mistake not playing you more. And I just want to say thanks for leading the way."

Andi felt embarrassed and tried to change the subject. "So your coach didn't give you a hard time about trying out for the team?"

"Not at all," Megan said. She lowered her voice for a moment: "Honestly, we're not very good. We're like you, oh, two, and one, but our tie was zero–zero. We've only scored one goal all season."

Andi thought that might be encouraging. Before

she could point out that her team had been out-scored 13–4 in three games, she heard a sharp whistle. Coach J was waving his players to the sideline to get ready to start the game.

"Gotta go," she said. "Nice to meet you. Good luck today."

"You too," Megan said. "Maybe we can exchange cells after the game."

"Sounds good," Andi said, and jogged over to join her teammates. Coach Johnston had his hands on his hips when she arrived a few seconds after the others. "You here to socialize or play soccer, Carillo?" he asked.

"Coach, she just came over to say hello . . ."

"Save it for after the game," he said. "If you're here to compete, fine. If not, you can go on home right now. You want to play or not?"

"I want to play, Coach."

"Fine."

Andi felt her face burning with embarrassment and anger. Prior to their previous games other members of the team had occasionally stopped to talk to opponents they knew for one reason or another. Apparently it was okay for the boys but not for the girls.

She took her place on the bench as the game started. Jeff sat next to her.

"Just when you think he's backing off on acting like a jerk, he goes and proves again that he's a jerk," Jeff said. "Don't let it bother you."

"How can I not?" she said. "He's the worst kind of bully because he picks on people who can't defend themselves—which I can't because he's my coach. The worst part of it is, if I just say, 'The heck with you,' and walk away from this team, he gets what he wants."

Jeff didn't have an answer for that one. She was right.

It was 0–0 midway through the first half when Coach J subbed for the first time. Four starters were pulled and four subs went in for them. The only sub who didn't get into the game was Andi.

As play resumed after the subs had gone in, Coach J walked over to where she was sitting. "Assuming you've figured out that this isn't a social hour by halftime, you'll get in then," he said.

He didn't give Andi a chance to respond, turning his attention back to the field. It was probably a good thing, Andi thought, that she hadn't had time to say anything. It only would have gotten her into more trouble.

Megan Tway had been right about her team: They weren't very good. But Merion didn't exactly look like an English Premier League team, either. The ball seemed to pinball back and forth in the middle of the field, neither team able to mount much of a scoring threat.

Finally, with about two minutes left before halftime, Mike Craig and Jeff maneuvered into scoring territory. Jeff, who was playing midfield with Zack Roth up front next to Ron Arlow, came down the left side and slid a pass to Craig, who got a step on a Main Line defender and bolted toward the penalty box.

Arlow was racing down the right side, calling for the ball, and Craig got it to him with only one defender between him and the goalie. The defender was Megan Tway.

Andi had noticed that when Arlow was one-on-one, he almost always made the same move: fake left, go right, and clear space for a right-footed kick or, if the defender completely bought the fake, keep going until the goalie was forced to make a move.

Arlow faked left: Tway stayed with him. As he moved right, she slid her left foot onto the ball as he tried to dribble it and punched it away from him. Then she raced after it while Arlow got his feet tangled and went down in a heap.

He came up screaming for a foul. "That's a penalty kick!" he yelped. "She tripped me!"

The referee had been right on the play. He shook his head at Arlow and ran downfield, following the ball.

Tway was about as good with the ball as anyone playing for Main Line. She got across midfield before Roth and Craig came to double-team her. She ran to the middle of the field, drawing the defenders to her, then slipped a pass to one of her teammates who was racing down the left side with no one from Merion near him.

He moved in on Bobby Woodward, made a surprisingly good fake, and when Woodward, anticipating a shot, dived at the ball, he maneuvered around him and easily kicked it into the empty goal.

Just like that, Main Line led, 1–0. That was the halftime score.

During the break, Andi found herself feeling angry and frustrated. Her team was trailing, and

Coach J had her tied to the bench for committing the crime of talking to an opponent.

Once again, she thought about what her dad had said before the season started: "We're talking about sixth-grade soccer, not the World Cup."

She realized someone was calling her name. It was Coach C: "You're in to start the second half," he said. He gave her a look that seemed to have an apology in it somewhere.

She didn't say anything. Playing well, she decided, would be the best response.

23

THINGS GOT WORSE, NOT BETTER. RON ARLOW DREW A YEL-low penalty card from the referee when he took Megan Tway down hard as she tried to clear a ball early in the second half. Tway got up after a minute, limping a little but insisting she was all right.

One of her teammates walked over to Arlow, pointed a finger at him, and said: "Do anything like that again and you'll be carried off the field."

Arlow laughed, but—not surprisingly—decided that was a good moment to move to the other side of the field as play resumed. Coach Johnston wasn't the only bully who was part of the Merion team. *And, like most bullies*, Andi thought, *he runs away as soon as someone stands up to him.*

A few minutes later, the same boy who had come after Arlow got past Mike Craig at midfield and moved into the penalty area. Unsure who should try to cut him off, both Danny Diskin and Ethan Lewis went after him. That left the other forward wide-open. Just as he was about to shoot, Jeff charged at him from behind and dived at the ball—a brave, if unwise move. The two players went down in a heap.

The referee, having already witnessed one dirty play by a Merion player, decided this must be another one. He came in waving his yellow card at Jeff and pointing at the penalty spot—indicating that Main Line would get a penalty kick, since the play had taken place inside the penalty area.

The call angered Jeff. "I went for the ball, not the man," he said to the referee, hands extended palms up to plead his case.

"One more word and you'll get a red card," said the ref, who apparently had seen enough of Merion's tactics.

Andi knew that a red card would mean that Jeff would be ejected from the game *and* would have to sit out the next game. Jeff knew it, too. He turned and walked away, mumbling to himself.

The referee put the ball on the penalty spot. Anyone on the field could take the penalty kick. Megan Tway was Main Line's choice.

"She never misses," one of the Main Line players said to Andi as everyone lined up. "Just watch."

He wasn't kidding. On a penalty kick, the goalie can't move until the ball is kicked. That means he has to guess which way the ball is going to go and hope he gets it right to have any chance at all.

Bobby Woodward actually guessed right—diving to his left. It didn't matter. Tway's kick went into the far corner of the net. Megan Tway had a strong—and accurate—leg.

"Best keeper in the world doesn't stop that one," Jeff said.

He was standing next to Andi, still shaking his head about the call.

"Don't worry about it," she said. "You went for the ball, and the guy went down. Wasn't your fault."

She patted him on the back. Then came her least favorite sound in the world: the sound of Coach J's voice.

"Carillo, Michaels, are you here to play or chat?"

Everyone was headed upfield for Merion's kick-off. The exchange had taken about a half second.

Jeff rolled his eyes as they ran toward midfield.

"Least he's consistent," Andi said.

Leading 2–0—and no doubt surprised by the margin—Main Line went into a shell defense, keeping eight or nine players back most of the time to keep Merion from getting any open space in the offensive area of the field.

Andi had the best chance to score midway through the second half when she tracked down a long pass from Diskin in the corner, cut around one defender, and found herself one-on-one with Megan Tway. Andi made a good fake to clear some space, lined up the kick, and thought for sure her shot was going to find the upper-left-hand corner of the goal.

But she had rushed it a little, and the ball clanked off the corner of the goalpost and bounced away harmlessly.

Merion kept pressing, pushing more and more players toward the goal. Arlow had a chance but shot the ball wide. Andi made another good move and got the ball to Jeff, closing in on the goal, but Main Line's goalie anticipated his shot well and made a diving save.

Jeff and the other Merion midfielders had pushed deep into the offensive zone to try to create a numbers advantage. That had led to Jeff's being open.

But when the goalie made the save, he quickly leaped to his feet and, with the Merion players still pushed up into their attacking zone, boomed a kick to midfield. Merion had only two defenders back and the Main Line midfielders had sprinted back while the Merion players were still trying to figure out how Jeff's shot hadn't resulted in a goal.

Main Line ended up with a five-on-two break. The same player who Jeff had taken down to create the penalty kick executed a neat give-and-go, and poor Woodward ended up with two Main Line players closing in on him with Merion's defenders sprawled helplessly on the ground after unsuccessfully trying to steal the ball.

That was the thing about defending in soccer: If you went for the ball and failed to get it, you usually left a teammate in trouble. In this case, that teammate was Woodward.

He tried to dive at the player with the ball before he could shoot. He simply slipped it back to Jeff's tormentor, who booted it into an empty net to make it 3–0.

That was the last goal of the game. All the air went out of the Merion players after Main Line's third score. The referee's whistle as the clock hit zero was merciful. No one in a Merion uniform wanted to spend any more time flailing helplessly.

As the players went through the handshake line, Megan Tway wrapped an arm around Andi. "Your coach is a piece of work," she said. "I'm not even sure why you want to play on his team."

"We're not very good, are we?" Andi said.

"I see some guys who have talent," Tway said. "You've got more good players than we do. But I don't see a lot of teamwork going on."

Andi knew she was right.

They were now 0–3–1 for the season. Walking off the field, she could hear Tway's words very clearly inside her head: "I'm not even sure why you want to play on his team."

She couldn't help but wonder the same thing.

24

JEFF WAS ANGRY WHEN THE GAME ENDED. HE WAS ANGRY that the team—himself included—had performed so badly. He was angry at Coach J for finding an excuse to not play Andi more. He was angry at the ref who had given him a yellow card for what he thought was a clean play.

He was even angrier when the kid he'd taken down introduced himself during their handshake. "I watch your dad on TV," the kid said. "I thought you made a good play on me—for what it's worth."

It was nice to hear but, ultimately, worth nothing. Even though no one had said anything to him, he knew he was steadily improving. He felt good about that, and he knew that—like Andi—he should be starting. But none of that changed the fact that the team still hadn't won a game.

He walked to the locker room with Andi and Danny Diskin. There was very little talk. The only thing that made this group a team in any way was that they were all wearing the same uniform.

Jeff was surprised when Coach J walked up from behind as they were about to reach the locker rooms and tapped Andi on the shoulder.

"You come inside for a minute with everyone else," he said. "You need to hear what I have to say, too."

He saw Ron Arlow look at the coach in surprise, but he said nothing.

"Everyone take a seat," Coach C said once they were all inside.

They sat in front of their lockers. Andi squeezed in between Jeff and Danny. Coach C stepped aside and let his colleague address the team.

"That was an awful performance," Coach J began.

Jeff looked straight down at the floor. He didn't want the coach or anyone else to see him rolling his eyes as the coach began to point fingers—again.

"That team had about three good players. The

best of them was the girl they had playing defense. But there's no way we should have lost that game, and we certainly shouldn't have lost it three–zip. I'm embarrassed and I hope all of you are, too."

Here Coach J paused. "That being said, I owe you all an apology. I've been so focused on proving I was right that this shouldn't be a coed team, that I haven't done a very good coaching job. You guys have spent more time fighting with one another than our opponents. That's mostly on me."

He looked at Andi. "I haven't always put our best players on the field." He pointed at Jeff. "You agree with me on that, Michaels?"

For a second, Jeff sensed a trap. But he answered honestly. "Yes, sir, I agree," he said.

Coach J swung his gaze to Arlow.

"What about you, Ron?"

"Sir?" Arlow said, baffled.

"Do you think I've done a good job getting our best players on the field?"

Arlow said nothing for a minute. The silence was deafening. "No, sir, I don't," he finally said.

"That ends next week," Coach J said. "Coach C and I will decide who starts and who plays together.

My first job as your coach is to see to it that all of you have fun playing soccer. My second job is to try to help you win games. I've failed miserably at both. I've created a toxic atmosphere. We're not a team, we're about five different cliques. That's on the coach."

He took a deep breath. "Any questions?"

Diskin's hand shot up.

"Should have known," Coach J said with a weary smile. "Yes, Diskin."

"Coach, what's a clique?"

Everyone laughed.

"Michaels, you tell him," Coach J said.

"It's a small group that sticks together and doesn't let anyone else into the group," Jeff said.

"Anyone disagree with that evaluation of this locker room?" Coach J asked.

"Yeah," Jeff said. "Don't you think it's more like six cliques?"

The tension broke. Everyone laughed again—really laughed.

"You might be right, Michaels," Coach J said. "I'll see you all Monday. We'll start over then."

He turned and walked out.

Jeff looked at Andi and Danny.

"What just happened?" he asked.

Diskin grinned. "I think you and Andi just became starters," he said. "And I think we just got better."

"A lot better," Mike Craig said, joining them. "Do you think we can start out Monday by electing a new captain?"

"Got any ideas?" Jeff asked.

"Sure do," Craig said. He put an arm around Andi, who blushed noticeably.

"I better get out of here before you guys start showering," she said.

Arlow—naturally—was already a step ahead. "Hey, Carillo," he said. "You think maybe you can give us some privacy?"

"Like I was saying," Craig muttered.

There was no election of a new team captain on Monday. But practice was noticeably different.

Andi and Jeff spent more time playing with the first team than with the second. Danny Diskin was restored to his spot with the first team for much of the afternoon.

Coach C was in charge for the day because, Coach

J explained, he had come up with an idea to change the way the team lined up. Instead of using a two-four-four formation—two forwards, four midfielders, and four defenders—he explained that they were going to try a three-four-three, which might make them a little more vulnerable on the back line but more dangerous near the goal.

"We need to score more," he said. "There's an old basketball saying that the best teams are 'hard to guard.' We need to be harder to guard. We've scored four goals in four games, been shut out twice. That's not good enough."

The front line for much of the day consisted of Arlow, Craig, and Andi—with Andi on the left, Arlow in the middle, and Craig on the right. Arlow said nothing about the new setup but was noticeably quiet throughout the practice.

When it ended, Coach J brought them all to midfield.

"I thought we looked good today," he said. "Coach C and I will talk tonight and we'll have the starters posted for you tomorrow when you get here for the game. We've got Malvern tomorrow and then the next two games are on the road. Malvern's two and oh in conference, so they're obviously pretty good. We'll need to play our best game of the season to have a chance to win. So let's be ready."

He looked at Arlow.

"Ron, bring them in."

Arlow looked about as eager to lead a cheer as walk on hot coals. But he walked to the midfield spot, put his arm up in the air and said, "Everyone come on in," with little enthusiasm.

Everyone walked into the circle and put their arms in.

"Beat Malvern," Arlow said, as if reciting the alphabet.

The response was considerably more enthusiastic. "Beat Malvern!" they yelled.

Everyone looked at the coaches, wondering if they would have any comment about Arlow's apparent disinterest. Neither said anything. Without another word, they all headed to the locker room.

25

AT JASON CRIST'S SUGGESTION, HE AND HAL JOHNSTON went to dinner. They drove into downtown Philadelphia and went to the Palm, the famous steak house on Broad Street, just a couple of blocks from City Hall.

"At the least, you'll get a good meal out of it," Crist had said when he suggested dinner at the Palm.

Johnston had seriously considered resigning from his coaching position after the loss the previous Friday. Walking off the field after the embarrassing 3–0 loss to Main Line, he had said to Jason, "This team will be better off without me. I'm going to quit and let you be the coach."

Jason hadn't been surprised. He knew how frustrated his friend had been with everything that had gone on, starting with Principal Block insisting he let Andi Carillo try out for the team. He disagreed with Johnston on the issue but knew his intentions were good.

"Don't do that, Hal," he had said. "At least take the weekend to think about it. Don't make a decision right now when you're upset."

Johnston had listened, telling the players he needed to do a better job as their coach rather than saying he was walking away. The two men had talked at length over the weekend.

Jason had known Johnston for five years—since he had come to teach at Merion Middle. Johnston had been there for seven years already, and since both were sports fans, they'd become friends quickly. Both had been excited when the Montgomery County public schools had announced they were going to start sixth-grade programs in sports for the first time: boys' soccer and girls' field hockey in the fall, boys' and girls' basketball in the winter, and boys' and girls' softball in the spring.

They had volunteered to coach right away—each receiving a small stipend every week for doing so. Because Hal had more seniority as a teacher, he'd been named head coach, with Jason as his assistant.

Jason had trouble understanding why the notion of a girl on his team bothered Hal so much. Perhaps that was because he had two teenage daughters who both played sports and Hal and his wife, Monica, didn't have children.

It wasn't generational. Hal Johnston was fifty-one; Jason was forty-eight. They had argued about the coed issue from the beginning. After Andi had played such an important role in salvaging the tie in the opening conference game against Ardmore, Jason had thought perhaps the issue was finally behind them: Andi needed to play for the team to have a chance to succeed. So, for that matter, did Jeff Michaels—he was clearly the team's most improved player up to that moment.

Then Hal had gone out of his way to find a reason to bench Andi for the first half against Main Line, and it had clearly affected the entire team. Jason

suspected that the only player who had any problem at all with Andi at this point was Ron Arlow
and even he—deep down—had to know she was
probably as good a player as he was. Arlow was
faster and stronger, but Andi had a better sense of
the game.

They met at the restaurant, each valet parking
his car. They ordered drinks after sitting down
and, following a brief silence, Jason decided to get
right to the point.

"So who are you going to start up front tomorrow?" he said.

Hal Johnston smiled. "In other words, am I
going to finally give in and start Carillo?" he
answered.

"And Michaels," Jason said.

Hal smiled. Or was it a grimace?

"I've given this a lot of thought. I'm never going
to stop thinking that boys should play against
boys and girls against girls. It's just the way I was
raised."

"Me too," Jason said. "But times change."

Hal held up a hand.

"I know that," he said. "But this is a little bit like

asking someone who has played golf right-handed his whole life to play left-handed. I'm trying, I really am, but it goes against all my instincts."

"You'd feel differently if you had a daughter."

"Maybe. But I don't. Look, though, I feel as if I've let these kids down. I wanted to coach this team to have fun and let them have fun. Forget the winning and losing, they're eleven years old. Sports should be fun. I didn't mean to do it, but I've taken that away from them."

"So fix it."

"How?"

"Start the eleven best players tomorrow. Put aside your early twentieth-century beliefs about boys playing with girls and start Andi. Stop holding a grudge against Michaels and start him, too— he's earned it."

He paused, thinking. "And the next time Ron Arlow says or does something stupid—no matter who it's directed at—bench him. Send him—and the other players—a message that treating other people badly won't be tolerated. Like you said, we're playing for fun."

Johnston took a sip of his wine and picked up a pickle and began cutting it up.

"I'll say one thing about you, Jason. You *sound* like you know what you're talking about."

Jason smiled. "I have no choice," he said. "I have teenagers."

When Jeff arrived at the locker room door the next afternoon, he found Andi sitting on the bench outside the door, already in uniform.

"You need me to go inside and check the lineup?" he asked.

She shook her head and smiled. "Nope," she said. "Coach C already told me. I'm starting up front with Arlow and Mike Craig. And you're starting at midfield."

Jeff almost felt like dancing for joy. *Finally!* he thought.

He had another question.

"Diskin?" he asked.

"Starting, too," she said.

Jeff punched a fist in the air and said, "I better get moving."

Andi stopped him, putting a hand on his elbow. "Just for the record, I haven't said this before, but you deserve this, too."

"Thanks," he said, figuring he was grinning like it was Christmas morning.

He walked into the locker room and, naturally, the first person he saw was Ron Arlow. He braced, waiting for the verbal attack.

"Come on, Michaels, hustle up and get dressed," Arlow said. "We've got a game to win."

Jeff had no answer for that. He walked to his locker, took his uniform out, and started putting it on. Danny Diskin walked over.

"You saw the lineup?" he said.

Jeff nodded.

"We've got a chance now," Danny said. "I talked to Coach C. He said everyone plays, but the coaches are going to keep the best lineup on the field all day—including Andi."

"What do you think happened?" Jeff said. "I mean, Coach J said Friday he hadn't done a good job, but he didn't commit to anything yesterday other than playing three forwards."

Danny shrugged. "I don't know," he said. "Maybe it was like he said, he realized he wasn't doing a good job. Maybe Coach Crist talked some sense into him."

"Or maybe he just got tired of losing," Jeff said.

Danny smiled. "Well, that's something I think we can all agree on. Even Arlow."

Jeff knew Danny was right. Everyone was tired of losing. Even Arlow.

26

RIGHT FROM THE START THAT AFTERNOON, MERION WAS A different team.

Sure, it was partly the lineup change. But it was also the attitude.

Every Merion player—including Ron Arlow— seemed to have an extra bounce in his or her step; seemed to have an extra gear to get to loose balls; seemed to have an enthusiasm that no one watching them play had seen in their first four games.

It was as if they had invisible jet packs inside their uniforms.

The Malvern players were caught off guard. All they knew about Merion was that they were three-time losers and had gotten shut out the previous Friday by a Main Line team that Malvern had beaten 4–0 in their conference opener.

For the first time all season, Merion scored the first goal of the game. It came when Zack Roth took off on a run down the right side and fed the ball to Arlow, sprinting up the middle of the field.

Arlow was Merion's fastest player, and he was behind the Malvern midfielders in an instant, fast enough to go by them, skilled enough to keep the ball on his foot as he did.

As the defenders tried to close on him, he faked as if to pass to Craig on the right and then dished to Andi, who was closing from the left side.

Andi one-timed the ball—not bothering to stop it with her foot but booting it as soon as it arrived. Malvern's goalie never even moved because the ball was past him so quickly.

Five minutes in, Merion led.

Andi ran straight to Arlow, pointing her finger and saying, "Great pass, Ron! Great pass!"

"Amazing shot," Arlow said, and, for the first time all season, the two of them exchanged a hand slap.

The goal seemed to get Malvern's attention. The

game settled into a two-way battle, both teams making runs into the offensive zone, both defenses coming up with answers.

Then, with a little more than a minute left in the first half, Jeff made a steal at midfield and, seeing Andi open on the left, got her the ball. Andi streaked into the penalty area and was about to pass the ball to Arlow when she was taken down—hard—by a Malvern defender.

The referee raced in waving a yellow card and pointing to the penalty spot. Several Merion players charged the Malvern defender, who had also tumbled to the ground.

"My bad," he said, getting to his feet. "Honest."

He put out his hand. Andi accepted it. Everyone in Merion blue-and-gold pulled up.

"Just watch what you're doing," Mike Craig said.

The Malvern defender nodded. "Just trying to stop her from scoring, guys," he said. "Not easy, you know."

Jeff saw Craig and Andi smile at the comment. The referee had picked the ball up and placed it on the penalty spot.

"Okay, Merion," he said. "Who's taking this?"

Everyone looked at one another. This was the first penalty kick they'd been awarded all season.

"Andi should take it," Craig said. "She's the one who got taken down."

Andi shook her head. "Ron's got the strongest leg," she said. "Let him take it."

The clock was under twenty seconds. If they didn't get the kick off by the time it hit zero, they'd lose it.

From the sidelines, Coach J was yelling. "Someone take the kick! Arlow, you're the captain, decide!"

"Andi, take it," Arlow said.

The referee was lining up the players on both teams. The clock ticked under ten seconds. No time to argue anymore.

Andi lined up. The referee blew the whistle. Andi kicked the ball at the exact spot where the goalie had been standing. He had taken a dive to his left, anticipating her lefty kick going in that direction. The ball hit the net as the clock hit zero.

It was 2–0, and Andi had scored both goals.

They raced to the sideline—almost as one—for the halftime break. *This*, Jeff thought, *is fun*.

* * *

The second half wasn't without nervous moments.

Malvern made some adjustments and became much more aggressive, taking chances by pushing extra players into the offensive zone. As a result, Merion had some chances with odd-man rushes but couldn't convert.

Malvern finally broke through on a corner kick. The ball was kicked into the goal area, and a scramble for it ensued. Somehow it ended up on the foot of one of the Malvern players who was wide-open. He kicked it into an open corner of the net, and with ten minutes still left, the margin was 2–1.

"We've got to stay aggressive," Coach J said as they were lining up for the kickoff. "Don't let them back us up."

He pointed at Jeff. "Michaels, you get a chance to move up, you take it."

Andi and Jeff had played almost the entire game—rested, as was required by the rules, for five minutes apiece early in the second half.

Coach J's strategy paid off. With Malvern pressing for the tying goal, Bobby Woodward made a save on a weak shot and quickly threw the ball up the sideline to Jeff, who took off, pushing up with the ball so he became—in essence—a fourth forward.

The Malvern midfielders scrambled to get back, but Jeff had enough speed to get past them and pass the ball to Craig, who moved to the middle of the field and was about to tee up a shot when Arlow screamed, "Mike—Andi!"

Craig looked up and saw her cutting in from the left side completely unchecked. The defense had crowded the middle of the goal area and had, for an instant, forgotten about her. Craig slid the ball to the left winger, and she blasted it as soon as it arrived on her foot. The goalie actually guessed right and got a hand on the ball, but he couldn't stop it, and it deflected off his hand into the top of the goal.

All four Merion players who had been involved in the play had their arms in the air, and they raced into a group scrum while the rest of the team came up the field to join the celebration.

"Great pass!" Andi said, hugging Craig.

"Great eyes by Ron!" Craig replied.

Andi turned to Arlow, and they hugged—sort of—each throwing one arm around the other.

Jeff loved the entire thing—except maybe for the Andi-Craig hug. He understood it, but, being honest, he could have lived without it.

After all, he *had* started the play. Just then, Andi spotted him and gave him a hug, too. That was at least as cool as the goal.

27

THE THIRD MERION GOAL DEFLATED MALVERN. WITH UNDER six minutes to go, the chances they could score twice weren't great, and their players knew it. The aggressive runs up the field that had helped them chop the lead in half all but disappeared. When Merion got the ball, the players were content to pass it back and forth, even if they weren't attacking the goal.

Neither team came close to scoring in the closing five minutes, and the final was 3–1. *Finally*, Andi thought, *we actually won a game.*

The celebration was pretty raucous. Even the coaches took part, high-fiving each player with

Coach C saying repeatedly, *"That's* the kind of soccer we want to play."

Ron Arlow and his buddy Mark Adkins gave Andi fist bumps, and Adkins said, "Nice playing, Carillo."

Arlow settled for the fist bump without comment. That was fine with Andi. He had already come a long way in his approach to her.

Their record was now 1–3–1 overall, but more important, they were 1–1–1 in conference play. That meant if they could continue to play this way they might still have a chance to win the conference championship. Malvern had been undefeated coming into the game. There had been only one other unbeaten untied team—that was King of Prussia–North—and Andi knew that Merion wouldn't play them until the last game of the season.

They went through the handshake line, the Malvern players still appearing to be a little bit shocked by the outcome.

Andi felt very good about things as they all walked off the field. She was surprised when Arlow jogged up and walked beside her.

"You got a minute?" he asked.

"Sure," she said, sensing a big moment.

They walked in the direction of the girls' locker room to put some space between them and the rest of the players. Andi noticed Jeff pausing to see what was up but waved at him to keep going.

He waved back and turned toward the boys' locker room, glancing over his shoulder. Arlow waited until he reached the steps and started down them.

"Look, I want to be clear on where you and I stand because we're the two best players on this team," he said.

Not exactly modest, Andi thought, *but okay*.

"I'm going to do everything I can to help us win, and if that means passing the ball to you when you're open or crediting you when you make a good pass, I'm okay with that."

Andi felt a *but* line coming. She was right.

"But I don't want you to think that means I feel any different about a girl being on a guys' team than I did during tryouts. And don't think Coach feels different, either. He's just accepted that, like it or not, we're better with you on the field. I've accepted that, too. But my boys Mark and Ethan got benched today because Coach started you and Michaels."

"Jeff deserved to start," Andi said, feeling herself get angry.

Arlow waved a hand. "Maybe," he said. "And I *know* you deserved to start. I'm telling you I get that. But I'm still loyal to Mark and Ethan, and I don't feel good that they aren't starting. Doesn't mean I'm not going to do everything I can do to win no matter who's on the field. But let's not confuse being teammates with me being a cheerleader in the Andi Carillo Fan Club or asking you to the Halloween dance, which about half the guys on the team including your boyfriend Jeff probably want to do. You got that?"

Halloween dance? Where had that come from?

Andi gave him her best smile. "Ron, I wouldn't have it any other way," she said.

If Arlow picked up on her sarcasm, Andi didn't stick around to find out. She turned and walked away.

"Why do you think he let you take the penalty shot today?" Jeff was saying on the phone that night.

Andi had called him because she figured he should know what Arlow had said.

Andi had thought about that while showering. "We were up by a goal and I think he thought I'd make it. But if I'd missed, then it would have made me look bad. If he takes it and misses . . ."

"Right," Jeff said. "You make it, we're up two–nil, and he looks like the good guy for giving you the kick. You miss and he's still the good guy, but you have to deal with the embarrassment of missing."

There was a long pause. Andi wanted to say something about the dance—which was the week after the season ended. She hadn't really given it much thought until Arlow had brought it up after the game.

What if Ron was right? The last thing she wanted was some stupid dance becoming a thing between her and Jeff.

She would worry about that later. There was still plenty of soccer season left.

28

THERE WAS NO GAME FRIDAY BECAUSE THEY HAD A BYE, BUT in practice before their next game the following Tuesday, Coach J didn't mention to the team that their opponent, Gladwynne, was winless and had scored a total of two goals. That came up later, after Merion had thrashed Gladwynne 5–0 in a game in which all sixteen players got to play at least a half.

Gladwynne, Jeff noticed early, didn't even have a full complement of players. When the game began, there were only two players in uniform on the sideline in addition to the eleven starters. They had one player who looked like he'd played soccer before: one of their midfielders, who could control the ball well and get past defenders. But once he gave up the ball, none of his teammates had much of a clue what to do with it.

Arlow scored a hat trick—three goals, just as Andi had done against Malvern. Jeff knew the phrase from going to hockey games with his dad. When one of the Flyers scored three goals, all sorts of hats would appear on the ice, tossed from the stands. Jeff had no idea where they came from—he never really noticed anyone wearing a hat—but they magically appeared.

Jeff's dad explained to him that this was an old-time hockey tradition that actually had started in cricket—the British version of baseball—when a batter took three straight wickets. Jeff had no clue what that meant, but his dad explained that when someone took three straight—apparently a rare occurrence—he was presented with a hat. This led to hockey fans tossing hats onto the ice in honor of three goals and, later, three goals in soccer being called a hat trick for the same reason.

It was rare in hockey and even more rare in soccer, especially at the professional level, where three goals *total* in a game was often considered a lot.

No one threw any hats at Arlow, but he was clearly pleased with having accomplished the feat. Roth scored a goal, and so did Diskin—coming up from midfield—his first of the season. Andi had two assists in the first half, which ended with Merion up by four. Then she and Jeff sat out the entire second half.

"Home sweet home," Jeff said with a grin as they sat and watched.

Andi shrugged. "We're not needed," she said.

Jeff nodded. "But Arlow's still out there. Roth, too."

"I know," Andi said. "But we're winning, and you and I are starting. That's a long way from where we were a few weeks ago."

It was after the handshakes that Coach J let the players know how unimpressed he was with their impressive victory.

"That's the weakest team we're going to face," he said. "I'm sure you all figured that out pretty quickly. They aren't going to win a game. I was happy with the way you took control of the game quickly, but the fact is if we kept playing for another hour, they probably wouldn't have scored. So enjoy the win. There's an old saying in sports that you never throw one back. We'll take it.

"But Friday we're going to play at Cynwyd." He held up his phone. "I just got a text from their coach telling me they beat Malvern today. That means they've got the same record as us and they beat a team we surprised last week."

He paused. "Their best player missed their first two conference games because he was hurt—that's probably why they lost badly to King of Prussia–North. He's back now, and they will probably be the best team we've faced, at least in conference, so far.

"But we're also a lot better team now than we were at the beginning of the season. We win this game and we'll put ourselves in position to have a chance to win the conference. We lose, well, we're out of it. So come to practice tomorrow prepared to really get after it. We'll need to play our best game of the season on Friday."

He turned, started to walk away, then thought of something and came back. "Good win today. Ron, get 'em in for a cheer."

Arlow did as he was told, and Jeff found Andi and Diskin walking off the field.

"He's just full of joy, isn't he?" he said.

Andi smiled her smile. "He's not wrong," she said. "That really wasn't a very good team, was it?"

"They could have used a couple of girls, huh?"

Jeff looked behind them and saw Arlow jogging up.

"Actually, they probably *could* have used a couple of girls—especially if they were half as good as Andi," Diskin said. "I hear that Cynwyd has two girls and they're both really good."

"One of them is their goalie," Andi added.

Jeff had heard none of this. Apparently neither had Arlow.

"Where'd you hear that?" Jeff asked, clearly surprised.

"There's a website for the conference that some of the parents set up," Diskin said. "It has the rosters and leading scorers for each team. Of course you wouldn't know that, Arlow, because that would involve reading something."

"Well, guess we're in trouble on Friday then," Arlow responded, "since they've got two girls to our one."

He jogged off without waiting for an answer.

"Every day around here is just nothing but

yucks," Diskin said. "Between him and the coach, there's no enjoying anything."

"Can't believe he didn't know about the website," Andi said. "I figured he'd been on it every night looking for his name."

"He will now," Jeff said. "Especially after the three goals today."

He didn't mention that he'd be checking the site for the first time that night himself.

Andi was heading for the girls' locker room. It was the first week in October and, even at five thirty, Jeff could feel a chill in the air. Which reminded him that the Halloween dance was a little more than three weeks away.

He wanted to say something about it to Andi, but she was turning away. And Diskin was standing right there.

Not now, Jeff thought. But soon. Before someone else—like Mike Craig—asked first.

29

ANDI WAS HAPPY TO SEE BOTH HER PARENTS WAITING FOR her when she came out of the locker room.

Since her mom wasn't in the middle of a case, her hours these days were flexible. Her dad's hours were almost always flexible—which was why he worked at home at night a lot.

"Great win, Andi!" her mom said.

Her dad wasn't quite as enthusiastic. "Why didn't you play at all in the second half?" was his opening comment as they walked to the car.

"Dad, we were up by a bunch, and Coach J wanted to play some of the other guys."

"I didn't see Ron Arlow come out," her dad said as he chirped open the car doors.

"You sound like Jeff," Andi said. "And, by the way, he didn't play in the second half, either."

Her father said nothing for a moment as they all climbed into the car.

Just then, Andi's phone pinged with an incoming text. It was from Jeff.

My dad wants to come to practice tomorrow to do follow-up story. You OK with that?

Andi read the text to her parents.

"What do you think?" she asked. She was wondering if the presence of the TV crew might upset Coach J . . . again.

"Ask him why his dad wants to follow up," her father said.

Andi did. The answer returned quickly, and Andi relayed the message: " 'Lots of viewers have apparently asked what's been happening since you were put on the team' . . . Even his bosses!"

When Andi read the answer to her parents, they both nodded, and her dad said, "Sure, do it. I'm betting Coach J will put a positive spin on what's happened. Might even take credit for being so open-minded."

They all had a good laugh at that one.

* * *

Tom Michaels and his camera crew were waiting on the practice field the next day when Andi arrived.

"We're going to talk to your coach first," he explained. "He said he'd be here at three fifteen—which is one minute from now. That should give us a few minutes to talk to you before practice at three thirty."

That was fine with Andi. She thought it was a good sign that Coach J had agreed to talk.

Except he didn't show up at three fifteen. He walked onto the field ten minutes later, and Andi could see him waving Mr. Michaels and the crew away.

"Not now," he said. "I have a practice to run. I'll try to make some time when we're finished."

Jeff and Danny Diskin were standing next to Andi as they waited for the coaches to walk over to start practice.

They could hear Tom Michaels—clearly upset—talking to Coach Johnston.

"We got out here at three o'clock to set up because you said you wanted to do this before practice," he said. "What happened to, 'I'll be ready to go at three fifteen'?"

"Got tied up, sorry," Coach Johnston said. "You don't have to stay if you don't want to. Your call."

Now Andi got it. Coach J was hoping Mr. Michaels would get upset and leave without doing the story at all.

"What time is practice over?" the reporter asked.

"Can't promise an exact time, depends how the kids are feeling," Coach J said. "Usually around five."

"We'll be back," Mr. Michaels said, and signaled his camera guy to take down the camera and tripod that had been set up. He walked over to where Andi, Jeff, and Danny were standing.

"In my business we call this being slow-played," he said, not breaking stride because Coach J was whistling the team to the center of the field.

The practice was a difficult one. The usual stretching and calisthenics went longer than usual. Then came fifteen minutes of keep-away with one then two players inside small circles of players. Then there were some ladder sprints—for no apparent reason. Finally, just before four, they split up into teams to scrimmage. Andi, Jeff, and Danny were all back with the second team.

The three of them exchanged a look as they were lining up. They all knew the reason for the punishment.

At about four thirty, Mr. Michaels and his cameraman were back on the sidelines. Andi was relieved. The thought had occurred to her that Coach J might cut practice short so that he'd be gone when they returned.

Since that tactic wasn't going to work, he dragged the practice on an extra ten minutes and then spent several post-practice minutes reminding them of the importance of Friday's game. Jeff's dad's cameraman had been shooting the last few minutes of practice, and he then videoed the post-practice talk. If Coach J cared, he didn't show it.

Finally they were dismissed with a reminder that they'd have a short practice on Thursday— mostly drills; not much running—to be fresh for Friday.

As Coach C collected practice balls and other equipment, Coach J walked directly to Mr. Michaels and said, "Ready?"

"Need about two minutes to get the camera set up," Mr. Michaels said.

"You've got one," Coach J said.

Andi was reminded of something her father had said back in mid-September. "Who does this guy think he is, Bill Belichick?"

Apparently he did.

When the interview started, Coach Johnston was all smiles and sunshine. He was glad that he'd been ordered to put Andi on the team, he said. She was a good player and—with his encouragement— her teammates had accepted her.

Andi almost choked when she heard that answer.

"Why was Andi on the second team for most of today's scrimmage?" Mr. Michaels answered.

"We're going to need all sixteen players to contribute on Friday," Coach J said. "I wanted to see different players in different roles today. We had an excellent practice."

He'd been ready for that one.

"What do you think your record would be right now if Andi Carillo wasn't on your team?" Mr. Michaels asked.

He didn't seem as prepared for that one. He

thought for a moment and then finally said, "It would be two, three, and one."

"That *is* your record," Mr. Michaels said.

"I know," Coach J said, not even the hint of a smile on his face.

30

THE PIECE RAN ON THURSDAY NIGHT AND WAS BILLED AS "Tom Michaels's update on Philadelphia's feel-good story of the fall."

In addition to Coach J, Andi, Danny, and Mike were interviewed on camera. Andi kept it upbeat, saying she was thrilled with the way her teammates had accepted her. She didn't bring up Ron Arlow or his pals. Diskin and Craig were both asked what the team's record would be without Andi.

"We'd be one and five," Diskin said. "The only game we wouldn't have lost would have been against Gladwynne."

Craig took it a step further. "The only game we *might* have won was Gladwynne," he said. "Even that wouldn't be a lock without Andi. And no way do we beat anybody else."

Jeff wished he'd had the chance to say something like that but, of course, he wasn't part of the piece.

Wrapping it up on camera, his dad tagged the piece by saying, "Michael, this team's come a long way since September but still has four games to play. We'll see how things turn out."

"We sure will, Tom," said Barkann back in the studio when he came on camera. "I think we're all Merion fans right now—and especially Andi Carillo fans."

The next day dawned bright, beautiful and chilly—a perfect October day for football—and, Jeff thought—for soccer.

Everyone was quieter than usual during warm-ups. There was little of the rah-rahing that normally went on prior to a game. It was as if the players had taken Coach J's words to heart about the importance of what was to come and the quality of the opponent.

Cynwyd did have two girls on the team. Jeff had

figured out how to find the conference website and had learned that Patrice Merkens was the goalie and Carla Hastings not only played forward but was also the team's leading scorer with six goals and six assists.

She was impossible not to miss in warm-ups: She was very tall, and her long blond hair was tied back in a ponytail.

Diskin walked over to Jeff during a lull, hands on hips. "If you can't get Andi to go to the dance with you, I'll ask her," he said.

Jeff had made the mistake of telling Danny he was thinking about asking Andi to the Halloween dance. Now, he regretted it. On the other hand, Danny wasn't wrong.

Coach J started the same lineup as he had started in the previous two games. It was one thing to play mind games in practice, but with the season at stake, he couldn't afford to not have his best lineup on the field. So Jeff and Andi were on the field from the get-go.

Both teams were cautious in the first few minutes, no one wanting to make the first mistake. Unfortunately, it was Jeff who made the first one.

Trying to move the ball past midfield, he thought he spotted Zack Roth open to his right. But he hadn't noticed one of the Cynwyd defenders sneaking up from his left-back position. The defender darted in front of Roth to intercept Jeff's pass and took off in full flight with the ball.

Everyone on the Merion side had been going forward. Now, they were caught flat-footed as the defender pushed way ahead. Jeff tried to scramble back to cut him off, but just as he closed on him, the back-turned-forward crossed the ball to Hastings, who was unmarked with Merion's defenders trying to keep the ball away from the other two forwards who were both in the penalty area.

Hastings reached up with her left foot to knock the pass down, gathered it, closed in on the penalty area, and before any defender could make a move at her, blasted a right-footed shot that flew over Bobby Woodward's dive and found the left corner of the net.

Jeff stopped running and stared for a moment. It was easily the most impressive goal he'd seen all season, a play worthy of a pro—seriously, he thought, a Philly Union player would have been proud of that shot. It was hard to believe that Hastings was a sixth grader.

The Cynwyd players raced to celebrate with Hastings. Jeff glanced at the scoreboard: Twelve minutes were left in the half and Cynwyd led 1–0. He mentally kicked himself for the mistake.

He was still shaking his head when he heard the voice of the referee.

"Hey, number ten!" he said, and tilted his head in the direction of the sideline.

Coach C, who signaled subs into the game, was holding up a large piece of cardboard with the number ten on it. That meant Merion was subbing and the player coming out was Jeff.

"Keep your head up," Coach C said to Jeff as he came off and Mark Adkins went in to the game in Jeff's place. "You'll be back in soon."

Coach J wasn't as encouraging. "How could you not see the defender sneaking up like that?"

"Sorry, Coach," was all Jeff could say in response. He knew Coach J was right—he'd made a mistake. But Cynwyd's players had made a terrific play to create the goal.

The rest of the half was scoreless, although Arlow beat the Cynwyd goalie with a shot from the left side of the box only to watch it ricochet off the goalpost and bounce away harmlessly.

Apparently Coach C's definition of "soon" was different than Jeff's, because he didn't play the rest of the half. At halftime, Coach J told the three starters—Jeff included—who had come out at different points during the first half that they were back in the game to start the second half.

"No mistakes!" he said, looking directly at Jeff. "They'll make one sooner or later. Next time Ron gets an open shot, I'm sure he'll bury it."

It wasn't Ron who got the first open shot in the second half—it was Jeff. About ten minutes in, he noticed the same Cynwyd defender sneaking up again, apparently intent on stealing another pass from him. For some reason, a quote from a famous basketball coach popped into his head—"I may be dumb, but I ain't stupid"—as a pass from Diskin landed at his feet near midfield. The same defender was creeping toward Roth, who at that moment appeared open. Jeff held on to the ball and then, as the defender got a little closer to Roth, yelled,

"Zack!" and made a move as if to pass it to him. The defender charged at Roth but instead of passing, Jeff raced directly into the hole the defender had vacated to run at Roth.

He had two steps on the guy, and the Cynwyd midfielders were scrambling to get back. Jeff moved into the offensive area with a four-on-two break—Andi left, Arlow middle, and Craig right.

He waited for another defender to come and stop the ball—that was the cardinal rule of defense in soccer, as in basketball: Stop the ball first.

But no one came toward him. One defender stayed with Andi, another with Arlow, while the goalie leaned to her left to get an angle on Craig, figuring the ball would go to the open player.

Still unmarked, Jeff crossed into the penalty area. He looked at Craig for a moment, and when he saw the goalie make a move in his teammate's direction, he took another step in the direction of the goal. Reminding himself not to try to kill the ball as he tended to do when shooting, he unleashed a shot aimed at the right corner.

The shot was perfect; the goalie had no chance to get back. The ball hit the back of the net for

Jeff's first goal of the season. More important, it was Merion's first goal of the game, and it tied the score.

Jeff threw his arms in the air while Andi and Craig raced to congratulate him. Arlow was slower getting there but put his hand up for a high five.

"You gave them a goal, now you got us one," he said. "Nice recovery."

That was as close to a compliment as Arlow had in him. *Good enough*, Jeff figured. He ran back upfield and glanced at the scoreboard. The clock had just ticked under fifteen minutes.

31

NOT MUCH HAPPENED IN THE NEXT TEN MINUTES. FOR A while it appeared that both teams were content to play for a tie. It occurred to Andi as the clock wound down that a tie would keep Cynwyd's chances to win the conference alive but would probably doom Merion.

That would explain why both her coaches kept yelling, "Push up, push up!" at their players. Andi knew they were right.

When a Cynwyd shot from long range flew over Bobby Woodward's head and over the goal, the official blew his whistle to indicate that both teams wanted to sub. Coach J took Mark Adkins out and replaced him with Allan Isidro, who was probably the slowest player on the team, but also had the strongest leg. It wasn't an *accurate* leg, which was why Isidro played midfield. At his best, Isidro might be able to set one of the forwards up with a long pass.

While the subs were being whistled in, Andi ran over to Arlow and waved a hand at Craig, Roth, and Jeff. All three saw her and hustled over.

"We can't tie!" she said. "It's not good enough if we want a chance to win conference. We have to gamble!"

"We know that, Carillo," Arlow snapped.

"Shut up, Arlow; she's right," Craig said. "You better be ready. We've got to score."

Arlow was about to say something in response, but the whistle blew and they all ran back to their positions as Woodward prepared to put the ball back in play.

Andi noticed that Cynwyd clearly didn't want a tie, either. Even though it wouldn't doom them, it would damage them. Plus, they no doubt thought they *should* win.

Roth had just lost the ball trying to push it into the offensive zone, and Cynwyd was on the attack—all three forwards and all four midfielders pushing forward. The midfielder who had taken the ball from Roth had quickly passed the ball to Carla Hastings, who had come back to get the pass and now began roaring down the left side.

Cynwyd had numbers: Roth was behind the play after losing the ball and so was Isidro for the simple reason that he was slow. Andi made a split-second decision and sprinted as fast as she could straight at Hastings. She had the advantage of not being slowed by dribbling the ball.

Hastings was moving into position to either set someone up or attack the goal herself. Merion's defenders were cautiously staying back, afraid, no doubt, that Hastings would use her quickness to get past them.

Andi ran in a straight line at Hastings as she prepared to make a decision on what play to make. She wasn't even looking at her when she slid, feet-first, directly at the ball.

She felt the ball thump off her hip and saw it roll away. Then, she felt a foot slam into her head. She cried out in pain and rolled over, holding the spot where the kick had landed.

She didn't know it, but the loose ball had been scooped up by Bobby Woodward as it rolled away from Hastings—thanks to Andi's steal. She heard the whistle and, as she lay on her back, eyes closed, she heard a voice say, "Don't move; don't try to get up."

She opened her eyes and saw Carla Hastings kneeling over her, concern written across her face.

"I'm so sorry," she said. "I got you on my follow-through. I didn't mean it."

Andi just nodded. She heard more people coming. She had one thought: *I can't come out of this game.*

By rule, she had to come out. Since the referee had stopped play for an injured player, there was no choice.

Jeff had run in Andi's direction as soon as she went down, and he could hear Coach J demanding the referee give Hastings a red card—which meant ejection—for the play.

"Coach, I was right on the play," the ref said. "Your kid made a great play but ended up right in the path of a foot that was already in motion."

Jeff turned his attention to Andi. Coach C was on one knee talking to her.

"There's no rush," he said. "The ref has stopped the clock because you were knocked out."

"I wasn't knocked out, Coach," Andi insisted. "I'm okay. My head hurts, but I'm okay."

Hastings, who had been telling anyone who would listen that the kick was an accident, was standing next to Jeff and behind Coach C.

"She's right, Coach. She wasn't out. She opened her eyes right away."

"She could still have a concussion," Coach C said. He turned back to Andi.

"Who are we playing, Andi? What's the score?"

"We're playing Cynwyd, it's one–one, there are about four minutes left, and *I'm fine!*" She shouted the last two words.

Jeff almost laughed when she said that.

Someone else was now on the field, kneeling next to Coach C.

"I'm a doctor," the woman said. "Carla's my daughter." She looked down at Andi.

"Do you think you can sit up?" she asked her.

Andi responded by pushing herself up on her elbows and then sitting up.

"Dizzy?" the doctor asked. "Nauseous?"

"No and no," Andi answered.

"Okay then, we're going to help you up." She looked at Coach C and added, "Slowly."

Gently, they each took an arm and helped Andi to her feet. Those watching from the sidelines applauded. Hastings apologized again. Andi's teammates moved in to gently console her, but the doctor held up a hand. "She needs some space. Let's get her to the bench."

As Dr. Hastings and Coach C walked Andi to the bench, the referee turned to Coach J. "I'm going to need a sub," he said.

Coach J turned to Adkins. "Go for Andi," he said.

Slowly, everyone returned to the field. Jeff saw 3:59 on the clock. The referee tossed the ball to Woodward, blew his whistle, and said, "Let's play."

And so they did.

Andi desperately wanted to get back in the game. She sat on the bench, with Carla Hastings's mother on one side of her, Coach C on the other.

The doctor was asking her questions about what day of the week it was; how many fingers she was holding up; what had happened leading up to her getting kicked in the head.

She answered them all. "I'm okay," she said, feeling the bump on her head. "I've got a little bump, but I remember everything clearly. I don't have a concussion."

"Are your parents here?" Coach C asked.

"No," she said. "Both working."

"Can you name all your teammates for me?" Dr. Hastings asked.

Andi sighed. The scoreboard clock said there were less than three minutes to play. She went through the team, closing her eyes to visualize where the starters were at the beginning of a game. Then she listed the five subs.

"What do you think, Doc?"

It was Coach J, who had walked over to the bench.

"I *think* she's okay," the doctor said. "She hasn't missed an answer yet. If this were football, I'd say keep her out, but it isn't. The one thing I'd require, though, if you decided to let her back in the game, is she agree *not* to try a header."

"I promise," Andi said, feeling hope and relief.

"How certain are you she's not at risk?" Coach J asked.

"Ninety percent," the doctor said.

The two coaches looked at each other.

"What do you think, Jason?" Coach J said.

"I'm still nervous," Coach C said.

"So am I," Coach J said.

He leaned down and put his arm gently around Andi's shoulder. "Andi, I'm really sorry," he said. "My second most important job is to try to help you kids have fun and win. My most important job is to keep you safe."

Andi looked imploringly at Dr. Hastings.

She shook her head. "I'm sorry, too," she said. "I don't disagree with your coaches."

Andi looked at the clock again. Under two minutes. There was nothing to be done.

32

JEFF WAS ALSO FEELING PRETTY HELPLESS AT THAT MOMENT. He had glanced over to the bench and seen Andi with the doctor and the two Merion coaches and was pretty certain she wasn't going to talk her way back into the game.

Cynwyd had just had a corner kick that one of their strikers had headed wide of the goal, meaning Merion had another goal kick.

As Bobby Woodward was recovering the ball from behind the net, Jeff heard Arlow calling his name: not Michaels, but Jeff. Surprised, he ran in the direction of midfield as Arlow ran back to meet him. Arlow was waving his arms at Woodward to hang on to the ball for a moment.

Jeff was baffled. There were less than ninety seconds left; the last thing Merion needed to do was waste time.

"Quick," Arlow said. "Run back and tell Woodward to get the ball to Isidro. Allan will know what to do with it."

"But . . ."

"Just do it!"

There was no time to argue. Jeff ran as fast as he could at the baffled Woodward.

"To Allan," he said. "To Allan."

Instead of kicking the ball, Woodward flung a sidearm pass to Isidro. Because Cynwyd considered Jeff and Zack Roth the primary midfield threats for Merion, Isidro had some space.

He controlled the ball and then, without trying to take advantage of the open space in front of him to make any kind of run, he boomed a high, looping kick that seemed to stay in the air forever.

Jeff was running after the ball, but it came down just outside the penalty area and was instantly surrounded by players in both red and white, Cynwyd; and blue and gold, Merion. He saw Zack Roth kick it in the direction of the left corner. Normally,

Andi might have been there. Now, though, it was Mike Craig, and he had two defenders trailing him.

In the middle of the penalty area Arlow was making a run straight at the goal, arm in the air, screaming, "Now, Mike, now!"

Craig seemed to understand—and then he didn't. Instead of trying to cross the ball into the crowded penalty box, he flipped a short pass to Roth, who was charging up from behind the two-team scrum near the goal. Jeff was running to Roth's left as defenders came to meet him.

Roth waited until the last possible second, and then slid the ball to Jeff, who was running full speed—and gasping from all the running he'd done in the last sixty seconds.

"Shoot!" he heard Arlow scream, and he saw what looked like the entire Cynwyd team turning toward him. It occurred to him that Arlow had been bluffing when he'd called for the ball from Roth and, more important, *he was bluffing now.*

Jeff drew his leg back and saw Cynwyd players diving to try to block his shot. He didn't shoot. Instead, he controlled the ball with his left foot and then, with his right, he looped the ball with far more finesse than he thought possible to where Arlow was standing, to the right of the goalie. No one from Cynwyd was paying attention because they were all expecting Jeff to shoot.

Arlow quickly stopped the pass with his right leg, brought it down to his feet, and fired a shot aimed for the far corner of the goal. The goalie got a hand on it and it looked like it was going over the goal. At the last possible second, it ducked just below the crossbar and into the net.

Jeff heard himself screaming and looking at the clock all at once. It said fifteen seconds and was still ticking. There wouldn't be time even for a kickoff. He and Arlow ran straight into each other's arms like long-lost brothers.

"What a pass!" Arlow screamed in his ear. "I didn't think you had it in you!"

"Me neither!" Jeff yelled back. "Great thinking!"

Before Arlow could respond, the entire Merion team buried them in a dog pile. Jeff was kicked and pummeled and pounded on the back.

He couldn't remember ever feeling happier.

* * *

Andi didn't have a very good view of the play from the bench, but the reaction of her teammates told her what had happened.

She started to stand up, but Dr. Hastings, who was now alone with her, put a hand on her shoulder.

"Easy," she said. "I know you want to celebrate—I get it. But I need you to take it easy. They'll come to you—I guarantee it."

She was right. As soon as her teammates unpiled, they began sprinting in her direction. Dr. Hastings stood in front of her, hands up. "Whoa," she said. "Gentle, please."

"How about high fives?" Danny Diskin asked.

The doctor smiled. "How about fist bumps?" she said, but not too enthusiastically.

They all lined up to fist-bump her. Jeff cheated, sneaking in a quick one-armed hug.

Andi then joined the handshake line. Every Cynwyd player shook her hand and most said something about hoping she was all right. Carla Hastings gave her a quick hug, saying over and over again: "I'm so sorry."

"I know it was an accident," Andi said. "Don't worry about it."

Carla smiled. "I'll tell you what wasn't an

accident—the play you made. I had that thing lined up. No way your goalie would have stopped me."

Now Andi smiled. "I know," she said. "That's why I had to try to stop you."

They hugged again. "Hope you can play next week," Hastings said. "Good thing is, there's no game on Tuesday."

Andi hadn't thought about that. The next week was the midway point of the middle schools' fall semesters and most kids had midterm tests and papers due, so there were no games scheduled until Friday.

When the team gathered after the handshakes, Coach J had a smile on his face.

"That was the best game we've played so far," he said. "Note my emphasis on *so far*. We've got three to go and because we pulled this one out, we can still win the conference. We're going to need some help the next couple of weeks because I checked and King of Prussia–North won again today, so they're undefeated. We need someone to tie them or beat them, and we need to win the next two so we can play them for the conference championship.

"The important thing today, though, is you guys

figured out a way to come from behind and win. Michaels, Arlow—those were great goals." He turned to Andi and pointed to her. "But the real hero, fellas, was Carillo. If she hadn't come all the way back to take the ball away from that tall girl, we would've been done. Way to go, Andi!"

They all cheered for her—even Arlow.

Andi's head was still throbbing a little. But she felt great—absolutely great.

33

COACH C HAD CALLED ANDI'S MOTHER TO TELL HER WHAT had happened, and by the time Andi had showered and changed, she found her mom standing outside the locker room with him.

"Is it okay to hug you?" her mom asked.

"Of course, Mom," Andi said, embracing her mother. For some reason, she noticed while they were hugging that she was a little taller than her mom. She hadn't noticed that in the past.

"I just gave your mom a list of symptoms to look out for tonight—just in case," her coach said. "The doctor doesn't think there's much chance any of them will occur, but better to be prepared."

"Like what?" Andi asked.

"Nausea, dizziness, feeling drowsier than normal, lack of appetite. That sort of thing."

"Well," Andi said, "you don't have to worry about lack of appetite. I'm starving."

The two adults laughed.

"Good sign," Coach C said.

Andi's mom held up a card. "Dr. Hastings also gave us a number, to call a doctor at Penn who specializes in head injuries to athletes," she said. "She's already checked and Dr."—she paused to look at the card—"Hall can see you first thing in the morning."

Andi groaned. "In the morning? It's Saturday, I want to sleep in."

"You can sleep in on Sunday," her mother said. "No negotiating on this one."

Andi understood. She was enough of a sports fan to know how seriously people took head injuries nowadays. She really did feel fine but knew her parents would want to be certain she was okay.

Her mom thanked Coach C.

"You sure you're okay?" she asked as they walked to the car.

"I'm fine—really. Can we stop at McDonald's on the way home?"

Her mom grinned. "Sure. Let me call your dad and see if he can meet us there."

That sounded like fun.

Dr. Hall was very friendly and outgoing when he greeted Andi and her dad—who insisted on taking her downtown to Dr. Hall's office—the next morning.

But he was all business while running her through all sorts of tests and asking questions—both to her and her father.

Finally, after flashing various lights in her eyes, he said he had one more test he wanted to run.

"You pass this and I won't insist on an MRI," he said. "You flunk, we do an MRI."

Andi knew enough about an MRI—where people get shoved into a tube in order to take pictures of some part of their bodies, in Andi's case the brain—to know she didn't want one.

"What's the test?" she asked.

"This is phase two of what is now the concussion protocol given to football players," he said. "I'm going to tell you a few things. Then you're going to sit in here alone for ten minutes. Then I'm going to come back and ask you what you can remember about what I told you."

He looked at Andi and her dad. "You guys okay with that?"

"Why does she have to be alone?" her dad asked.

"Because I don't want you in here reminding her what we talked about," the doctor said. "It's not that I don't trust you but . . ."

"You don't trust me."

"Sort of," the doctor said. "If it were my daughter I wouldn't want her to need an MRI either . . . Ready?"

Andi nodded.

"Okay, here goes."

He began slowly telling her things, most of them simple: The Phillies were in second place and would be playing the Giants that night. Pause. The Eagles were 4–2 and playing the Packers the next day. In Green Bay.

"Now for some things you may not already know," the doctor said. "I graduated from West Point in 1981. I got my medical degree from Duke. My wife's name is Anne."

He paused again. "Last group," he said. "The

high temperature today is supposed to be sixty. My favorite sport is hockey. The first thing I noticed about you when you walked in were your blue eyes."

He stopped. "Okay, we'll be back in ten minutes. You can lie down here and close your eyes or sit in a chair and read one of our year-old magazines."

He left along with Andi's dad. She opted to lie down and close her eyes. She ran through what the doctor had said in her mind. She was about to start a second run-through when the door opened. The ten minutes had gone fast.

She sat up. "Okay," the doctor said. "What can you tell me?"

She ran through what he'd said—keeping them in order because it was easier that way. "Why?" she asked finally, "is your favorite sport hockey?"

He laughed. "Because I played it in college," he said.

He turned to her dad. "I think she's absolutely fine, but, obviously, keep an eye on her for any symptoms the next few days. And no soccer until Wednesday. If she's got no symptoms between now and then, let her go."

"But we have practice on Tuesday," Andi objected.

The team had Monday off, since there was no game Tuesday.

"You can miss one practice, Andi," her dad said.

"And be glad that's all it is," Dr. Hall said. "It looks like you got lucky."

Andi sighed. She knew arguing was pointless. And the doctor was right—she'd gotten lucky.

Jeff was relieved to hear that the doctor thought Andi was all right when she called him on Saturday afternoon.

"Missing one practice is no big deal," he said. "It's not like we don't all know our roles at this point."

"I'm just glad we don't have a game Tuesday," she said. "That would have been a big deal."

They talked for a while about Friday's win. "It's too bad your dad wasn't out there with a crew," Andi said. "He could have done another story just on that game."

No response.

"Jeff, you there?" she asked.

"Yeah, sorry," he said. "Just thinking it's a good thing we'll have you back when we play Blue Bell."

"Yeah," she said. "They must be pretty good. Their only losses are to King of Prussia–North and Cynwyd."

"At least we're playing them at home."

"Yeah, helps not to have to ride the bus, doesn't it?"

They talked for another fifteen minutes, and Jeff was still smiling when he hung up the phone.

34

WHEN ANDI WALKED ONTO THE PRACTICE FIELD ON
Wednesday, several of the boys who were already
out there stopped to clap for her and came over to
welcome her back.

Arlow gave her a wave but continued loosen-
ing up with his pals Mark and Ethan. That was
fine with Andi. The fact that they seemed to have
accepted her as someone who could help the team
was enough.

Practice was routine, although Andi—again—
spent time with the second unit. She had thought
those days were over, but for some reason Coach
J had decided her absence from practice Tuesday
was an excuse to limit her—at least in practice.

Coach C had called on Tuesday night to make certain there had been no setbacks and to be sure she'd be able to practice on Wednesday.

"Don't be too surprised if Coach J limits you a little bit," he had said. "Part of it is, he wants you to be careful. The other part of it you probably understand."

Andi was tempted to ask him to elaborate but decided there was no point.

They didn't practice for very long on Wednesday, and Coach J said that practice Thursday was optional, since he knew some of them had papers to finish and tests on Friday.

"We aren't going to do all that much anyway," he said. "Rest is as important as practice at this point in the season. Plus, I don't want some teacher telling me next week that one of you is flunking a subject and you can't play in one or both of our last two games. So only come tomorrow if you're comfortable you are in good shape with your schoolwork."

They all nodded and listened, and then everyone showed up on Thursday. The season would be over a week from Friday—unless they somehow won the conference and got to play one extra game.

No one wanted to miss a practice. It proved sixth-grade schoolwork wasn't that hard, Andi mused, voicing that thought to Jeff and Mike Craig as they walked off the practice field.

"Even for Arlow," she added.

They both laughed.

Andi wondered if she'd be in the starting lineup the next day or if Coach J would be up to his old tricks of keeping her on the bench until she was really needed.

Jeff provided the answer when they went out to warm up the next day, the coldest of the year so far. Halloween and the end of daylight saving time were a little more than two weeks away and Andi could already feel winter closing in. She hated the end of daylight saving time—the sun setting before five o'clock. It just felt so dark.

"Same starters as the Cynwyd game," Jeff told her. "I guess Coach knows there's no time to mess around with his silly biases right now."

As expected, Blue Bell was a tough out. Like Merion, Blue Bell had one girl on the team. Unlike

Andi, she played on defense, which meant that she and Andi came face-to-face with each other on a number of occasions.

They shook hands and introduced themselves just before kickoff—Andi glancing over her shoulder to make sure Coach J wasn't watching.

"Carrie O'Shea," the girl from Blue Bell said. "I've followed your story. I admire what you've done."

"No such craziness on your side?" Andi asked.

Carrie smiled. "None," she said. "It helps that my mom is the assistant coach."

They both laughed. Andi hadn't noticed that one of the Blue Bell coaches was a woman. Now she did.

The first half was scoreless. Each goalie made one great save. The Blue Bell goalie's save was on Andi, who had gotten a pretty lead pass from Arlow and cut into the box, Carrie O'Shea step for step with her. Andi pulled up, cut outside to clear space, and fired a shot she thought was headed for the corner.

But the goalie took a quick step, jumped, and managed to deflect the ball just over the top of the goal.

At halftime Coach J told them he was going to try something a little different in terms of subbing. Every player had to be on the field for at least five minutes and every player had to be off for at least five minutes.

Instead of taking the team's best players out one at a time, he decided to gamble and take the entire front line—Arlow, Andi, and Craig—out to start the half. His thinking, he said, was that Merion would just play to keep the score tied, and then the trio would come in with a few extra minutes of rest and jump-start the offense.

It sounded good in theory until Danny Diskin, perhaps a little overamped knowing his team needed to keep the score at 0–0, took down a Blue Bell player in the penalty box, leading to a penalty kick.

Blue Bell was the first team Merion had played whose players had their names on the back of their uniforms. It turned out that one of the parents worked for a company that sold sports gear and he'd gotten the uniforms custom-made.

As a result, watching from the bench with Arlow and Craig, Andi knew that the player Diskin had taken down was named Gibbons. He slammed the penalty kick past Bobby Woodward and, three minutes into the half, Blue Bell led, 1–0.

"Well, that strategy worked out well," Arlow said as the players came up the field for the kickoff.

"We have to wait two more minutes before we go back in," Craig said.

"He could put us back in now, then take us out for two minutes later," Andi said.

The conference assigned someone from a neutral school to every game to keep track of who was playing and who wasn't. She wondered if Coach J might try to get them back in a little earlier—take a chance on whether it would be noticed—but he wasn't looking in their direction.

"We'll just have to figure out a way to score twice when we get back in there," Craig said. "Simple as that."

Only it wasn't as simple as that. As if determined to make up for his mistake, Danny Diskin took off on a run down the right side after the kickoff, with Jeff racing alongside, closer to the middle of the field. Diskin dodged a Blue Bell player named Shuck with a sweet kick between the defender's legs and tapped a pass to Jeff, who looked like he was going to blast a shot from just outside the penalty area.

At the last possible second, though, Jeff pushed the ball left, to where Mark Adkins, playing up front in Andi's spot, had been left wide-open. The goalie had moved to his left in anticipation of Jeff's shot. Now, he dived back in the other direction, but was a split second late. Adkins's shot didn't have much on it, but he was close enough to the goal and open enough that it slid just past the keeper's reach and into the net.

Andi was stunned, not just that they had scored, but the way they'd scored. Jeff's improvement as a player from the tryouts until now was amazing. What's more, she'd have bet money that Adkins wouldn't have been able to find the net—even from five feet away. But he had.

Remarkably, the game was tied at one all. It had taken less than a minute for Merion to tie the score.

"Well," Arlow said, "I guess Coach did know what he was doing."

They all laughed.

Two minutes later, there was a dead ball and Coach J waved all three of them back into the game.

"It's up to us now," Craig said as they jogged onto the field, high-fiving the three players coming out.

Andi nodded. He was right. There were no excuses now. If they wanted any shot at a conference title, they had to figure out a way to win this game.

35

AS IT TURNED OUT, WINNING THE GAME WASN'T NEARLY AS difficult as Andi had thought it would be.

Perhaps giving up the tying goal so quickly took something out of the Blue Bell players. Or maybe it was the sight of Merion's three best scorers coming back onto the field right after that goal. But something seemed to go out of them during the final twenty minutes.

Arlow scored the go-ahead goal with just under ten minutes to play, on a pass from Zack Roth, who chipped the ball over all the Blue Bell defenders' heads to Arlow in the penalty box. Arlow timed his move perfectly so as not to be offside, gathered the ball in, dodged the goalie when he dived at him, and booted the ball into what had become an empty net.

Five minutes later, after Blue Bell had turned the ball over trying to push for a tying goal, Jeff sent Andi down the left side with a long pass. She dodged one defender and cut into the box. Before she could make a move, the other Blue Bell defender—Roberts—took her down hard, hard enough that the referee raced in waving a yellow card.

Although Andi popped right back up, Jeff and Craig came running in, clearly wanting a piece of Roberts for the hard tackle.

"What the hell do you think you're doing?" Craig yelled, pointing a finger at him.

"Playing soccer," Roberts answered. "What's the matter, I can't tackle her 'cause she's a girl?"

It was the referee who answered. "You can't tackle anyone that way," he said, digging into his uniform and pulling out a red card. "The yellow is for the tackle. The red is for your lack of sportsmanship."

He pointed to the sideline to indicate Roberts had been ejected.

The Blue Bell bench erupted. Both coaches, male

and female, charged onto the field, screaming at the referee.

"Red card for what?" the head coach yelled.

"For not admitting his tackle was over the line," the referee said. "I probably should have given him the red right away for the tackle."

The coach calmed down. He put an arm around Roberts and led him from the field without another word.

The Merion coaches had also come onto the field just in case a fight broke out.

"Andi, you okay to take the penalty kick?" Coach J asked.

"I got kicked in the shin, I'm a little sore," Andi answered. "Let Ron take it."

Coach J nodded.

Arlow was standing there, hands on hips. "You sure, Andi?" he said. "It should be your kick."

"Just bury it, Ron," Andi said.

He pointed a finger at her. "You got it," he said.

The referee whistled everyone back into place and put the ball down on the penalty spot.

Arlow waited for the whistle, then did a stutter-step approach and booted the ball as Andrews, the goalie, dived helplessly in the wrong direction. It landed cleanly in the net, for a 3–1 lead.

That was the game. Coach Johnston took Andi out a minute later because she was limping a little.

"We've got this," he said. "Get off your feet."

For the first time all season, Andi didn't mind being taken out of a game.

That was the last score before the final whistle. In the handshake line, Roberts apologized to Andi.

"Frustration play," he said. "I'm sorry about the crack about you being a girl. You're a great player."

"Apology accepted," Andi said. "Thanks."

The last player in the Blue Bell line was Carrie O'Shea. After they had shaken hands, she pulled Andi aside.

"Listen, I need to tell you something you may not know," she said.

Andi was puzzled.

"You guys finish the season next Friday against King of Prussia–North," she said.

"I know," Andi said.

"My mom just told me they tied today. That means if you guys win on Tuesday, you can win the conference by beating them. You win, you'll be tied at six, one, and one and you'll have the tiebreaker because you beat them."

Andi was still puzzled. She knew the math already. They had talked about it before the game. The news that Cynwyd had tied King of Prussia–North was important, but why was O'Shea explaining it to her?

O'Shea read her mind and got to her point. "When we played them, the entire game most of their players were yelling at me that I didn't belong on the field, that I needed to go play girls' sports with other girls or that I should be taking a cooking class."

"Seriously?" Andi said. She hadn't encountered anything even close to that until Roberts's crack about Craig being upset with his tackle because she was a girl.

"Very seriously," O'Shea said. "Apparently their coach makes your guy look like a leader of the Me Too movement. And the players take their cue from him. They went after me with dirty tackles a few times.

"If the game is to decide the title, it'll probably be worse. You need to watch yourself."

Andi was caught off guard by this news. She hadn't heard anything about it before now, but then again, why would she? It wasn't as if the conference website was going to talk about it.

"Thanks," she said finally, offering O'Shea a hand. "I appreciate the heads-up."

O'Shea smiled. "Sure," she said. "I hope you guys win both your games next week. I'd love to see you knock those jerks off their pedestal."

"Well, Cynwyd did its part today," Andi said.

"Yeah," O'Shea said. "I'll bet it just about killed KP–North to be tied by a team that has not one but two girls on it."

"Well, here's hoping we go them one better next week."

O'Shea grinned. "Make sure you win on Tuesday first. Friday won't matter unless you win that game. KP–North will beat Gladwynne easy."

Andi knew she was right. Unless Merion beat McKinley on Tuesday, Friday's game would be strictly for pride. She wanted it to be more than that.

* * *

Jeff was about to walk over to Andi when he saw she was in some kind of deep conversation with the girl who had played defense for Blue Bell.

He waited until they finished, standing at a respectful distance so it wouldn't look as if he was eavesdropping. When Andi shook hands with the girl, he waited until she walked over to him.

"What was that about?" he asked. "Female bonding?"

She gave him what was clearly a nasty look. "Really?" she said. "You too?"

He quickly backed off, a little surprised that she'd reacted so angrily.

"Kidding," he said. "So what was it?"

She sighed.

"According to her, KP–North's players and coach *really* don't like the idea of girls on the soccer field—at least not a soccer field with boys on it."

"How does she know that?"

Another look. "She played against them, remember?" Andi said. "There were all sort of cracks about girls belonging in cooking classes and a number of dirty tackles. Apparently the coach is even worse on the subject than Coach J. It's just never come up because they didn't have any girls try out for their team."

"So she was warning you about them?"

This time he got a nod—a major improvement.

"Exactly. Carrie says if we end up playing them for the championship, they'll probably be especially nasty and chippy."

"What's chippy?" Jeff asked.

"Trying to get away with dirty plays. Trying to start trouble," she answered.

"Well, unless someone beats them or ties them, that won't be a problem," Jeff said.

She put her hands on her hips. "Well, unless we lose Tuesday, it will be a problem," she said. "Cynwyd tied them today. Carrie's mom told her."

Jeff hadn't heard.

"Hey, you two, come on, everyone in the locker room."

It was Coach C.

"Wonder what this is about," Jeff muttered.

"Probably that KP–North didn't win today and we've got a chance now."

"A chance or a problem?"

She smiled and said, "Both."

36

ANDI WAS RIGHT. COACH J WANTED EVERYONE TO KNOW that King of Prussia–North had been held to a tie by Cynwyd that afternoon, meaning if Merion beat McKinley on Tuesday it would play KP–North for the championship the following Friday.

"We've come a long way after the way we started," he said. "You've won some very tough games and overcome a lot." He looked directly at Andi and Jeff. "Some of you more than others. I'm very proud of you—regardless of what happens next week."

He paused, and Jeff saw a rare smile cross his lips. "But I'd rather be proud of you for winning the next two games than losing them."

Everyone clapped when he was finished, and Andi headed for the door. She gave Jeff a wave as she left and said, "Have a good weekend."

Jeff waved back.

Danny Diskin sat down on the chair next to him. He had a wide smile on his face.

"You better do it soon," he said.

"Do what soon?" Jeff asked.

"Ask her to the Halloween dance."

"What are you talking about?" He stopped himself.

"Are you kidding?" Danny said, laughing. "You should see the look on your face whenever you talk to her. You might as well be wearing a sign that says, 'I'm in love with Andi . . .'"

Jeff punched his pal in the arm. "Shut up," he said, looking around, hoping no one else was listening.

"What, you think I'm the only one who knows?" Danny said. "Let me tell you something, pal, you better ask her soon, because just about every guy in this room is thinking about asking her—including me. Only reason it hasn't happened is because we're all just as nervous about getting turned down as you are."

"What about Craig?" Jeff asked.

"He's not nervous," Danny said. "Half the girls in the sixth grade have asked him."

"And?"

"He's told everyone he's not going to decide who he's going with until after the season's over."

"It's good to be king, huh?"

"Yeah, but you can still be Prince Charming if you get off your butt and do something. She likes you."

"How do you know that?" Jeff asked, feeling his stomach tying into a knot.

"Same reason I know you like her," Danny said. "I'm only eleven, but I'm not blind or stupid."

"So you think I should ask her," Jeff said.

Danny leaned forward and took Jeff's head in his hands. "Do you need me to hit you over the head with a hammer? Ask her!"

He got up, took off his shorts, wrapped a towel around his waist, and headed for the shower.

Jeff went with his dad to the Eagles-Giants game on Sunday. Because Jeff couldn't sit in the press box during the game, his father had gotten Jeff and his mom seats in the NBCSP box during the game.

His mom was going to meet him there just before kickoff. Jeff left early with his dad to hang out in the press box, just as they had done in September.

They had gotten something to eat and were looking for a table when they heard a voice calling their names: "Tom, Jeff—over here."

Jeff saw Ray Didinger standing up at a back table waving at them. Michael Barkann was sitting at the table, too, and so was a third person Jeff didn't recognize.

"Mike Vaccaro from the *New York Post*," Didinger said, introducing Jeff as he and his dad walked over. "Tom, I assume you know Mike."

"Of course I do," Tom Michaels said. "We sat together at the Army-Navy game here a couple of times."

"Best event in sports," Vaccaro said, smiling. "But Ray and Mike were telling me you were involved in a pretty good story of your own this fall, Jeff."

"How's the season turning out, Jeff?" Didinger asked. "Do I need to come and do a follow up?"

"Easy, Ray, I've got dibs on the story now," Jeff's

dad said. "Matter of fact, if the team wins its next two games, it'll win the conference. And Andi and Jeff have both become starters and played a key role."

"All thanks to NBC Sports–Philadelphia," Barkann said.

"I'm sorry," Didinger said, "but who wrote the first column?"

They all laughed. Didinger turned serious. "Actually, if you guys play for the title, that might be worth a follow up. The first column got more clicks than any non-Eagles story we've had all fall."

Barkann turned to Tom Michaels. "Us too, Tom?" he said.

"It's a Friday, which means high school football," Tom Michaels said. "Might be a tough sell with staffing."

Barkann waved a "forget it" hand in his direction.

"Playoffs don't start in football for two weeks. I'm assuming the game's in the afternoon. We can get a crew there, turn the piece around, and if we need to get someone to a specific game that night, we can do it."

"The game's definitely in the afternoon," Jeff said. "We don't exactly have lights on our field."

"Not quite the Linc?'" Barkann said.

"Is it at your place?" Didinger asked.

Jeff nodded. "We play at McKinley on Tuesday, then home to King of Prussia–North. They're five, oh, and one, we're four, one, and one. So if we both win Tuesday—and they're playing the worst team in the league—we would have to beat them Friday to tie."

"But Merion would have the tiebreaker because of winning head-to-head," his dad added.

"Sounds pretty dramatic," Didinger said. "If you guys win Tuesday, let me know. I'll be there Friday."

"Us too," Barkann said.

"You in charge of the assignment desk now?" Jeff's dad asked the TV host.

"Yup. I just now put myself in charge," Barkann said. "Any objections?"

"None here," the reporter said with a wide grin.

"Tell you what," Vaccaro said. "If you guys win Tuesday, I'll come down on the train from New York. It sounds like fun, and it's a talkie."

Jeff's eyes went wide. "You know that term, too?" he said. "I thought Mr. Didinger and my dad were the only ones old enough to know it."

"Hey," Didinger said. "Just because I was there when Franklin Field opened doesn't mean I'm old."

Franklin Field was the football stadium at the University of Pennsylvania. The Eagles had once played home games there years and years ago.

"Isn't Franklin Field like a hundred years old?" Jeff asked. He had gone to a couple of games there with his dad. It was definitely *old*.

"Opened in 1895," Didinger said. "But I was *not* there."

Everyone laughed. All Jeff could think about was how cool it would be to beat McKinley and play KP–North for the conference championship. They would worry about what Carrie O'Shea had told Andi on Friday when the time came.

37

PRACTICE ON MONDAY WASN'T VERY LONG. THEY HAD NOW
been playing together—including tryouts—for almost
two months and were full of self-confidence.

As Andi engaged in a passing drill with her fellow
forwards, Ron Arlow and Mike Craig, she couldn't
help but think how fast the season had gone, especially considering how much had changed from
mid-September to late October.

That included the weather. Coach J warned them
after practice that the predicted high for Tuesday
was fifty degrees and there was a good chance it
would be accompanied by a cold rain at some point
in the afternoon.

"Put on a warm layer under your uniforms," he said. "Not too much, you don't want to be weighed down, but an extra T-shirt or even two might be a good idea."

It wasn't raining when they got on the bus for the ride up to McKinley, but a cold wind was whipping around.

Andi was glad she had heeded Coach J's advice and dressed warmly.

"My dad says once the game starts, we won't notice the cold," Jeff said. "You get some adrenaline going, you forget about it."

"I hope he's right," Andi said. She was thinking she'd rather stay in the locker room during warm-ups to wait until the last possible second to go back outside.

McKinley was smack in the middle of the conference standings with a 3–3 record. They had lost to the three teams ahead of them—other than Merion obviously—and beaten the three teams behind them. So it was hard to know what to expect.

When the game started, Andi kept waiting for the adrenaline Jeff had talked about to kick in so she would warm up. It wasn't happening. By the ten-minute mark, she was literally shivering. And then it started to rain. *Just what we need*, she thought.

Both teams played as if all they wanted to do was get back inside. The game was sloppy and there were few scoring chances in the first half. The more it rained, the muddier the field became and the harder it got to cut and move, not to mention control the wet ball, which seemed to get heavier by the second.

It was scoreless at halftime, and both head coaches opted to take their teams in to the locker room to warm up a little, Andi included.

"I know it's tough out there," Coach Johnston told his team. "But it's just as tough for them. You have to forget the weather. There will be plenty of time to be warm and dry after we win the game."

Easier said than done.

The rain continued in the second half, cold, steady, and drenching. No matter how often the referee brought a new, dry ball into play it quickly became slippery and heavy.

Coach J kept changing the lineup, bringing fresh players in to try to give his team a boost. The

McKinley coach did the same. When Andi came out for her mandatory five minutes, Coach C told her not to sit on the bench but to keep moving to try to stay warm.

There was only one way to get warm: Go inside. That wasn't an option.

McKinley actually had the best scoring chance when Danny Diskin fell down in pursuit of a loose ball and one of their midfielders took off on a run all the way into the penalty box. He drew the defense to him, then slid the ball to the kid who was clearly McKinley's best player—a very tall striker who scared Andi whenever he touched the ball.

Now, he had a clear shot at Bobby Woodward, and Andi cringed as he lined up the shot. But the wet ball squirted off the side of his foot and rolled harmlessly wide of the goal. Everyone on the Merion side exhaled.

It was still 0–0 with the clock ticking under five minutes, and Andi was thinking the whole season was about to be wiped out by the rain, the cold, and the mud.

And then, luck intervened. Ron Arlow had rifled a long shot that had gone over the goal. That gave McKinley's keeper a goal kick, and everyone dropped back, anticipating a long boot.

This time, though, as he made his run to the ball, his left foot slipped and instead of hitting the ball solidly, he kicked it off the side of his foot. The ball rolled to his right, in the direction of Andi and one of the McKinley defenders, both of whom had been expecting the ball to fly to the midfield area.

The McKinley kid, who had marked Andi all over the field throughout the game, had turned his head as the goalie approached the ball. Andi hadn't, remembering something she had read once in a book about Johan Cruyff, who had been a huge star for the Dutch national team years ago.

"Never assume anything in football," Cruyff had said. "Never take your eye off the ball."

Which was why Andi was looking right at the goalie when he kicked the ball and saw it coming right at her as it squibbed off his foot and the keeper ended up facedown in the mud.

Andi stopped it with her left foot, quickly transferred it to her right and then back to her left, and was running at the goal before her defender knew what had happened. The goalie had sprawled in the mud as he flubbed the kick.

He was trying desperately to scramble to his feet as Andi ran toward the net. He was too late. For a split second, Andi had been tempted to kick the ball from outside the penalty box with the goalie still trying to get up. But she remembered what had happened to the McKinley striker when he tried to line up an open shot minutes earlier.

Instead, she sprinted around the goalie as he was getting up and attempting to dive in her direction. Then, having gone around him, she got to within five yards of the goal and easily kicked the ball into the empty net.

The goalie, having only grabbed hold of empty air, lay with his face in the mud, pounding his fist in frustration. Andi had her arms in the air as much in surprise as celebration.

"That was the luckiest goal ever," the goalie said as he pulled himself to his knees.

"Still counts, doesn't it?"

Andi laughed. The comment had come from Arlow, who had raced in from behind and also had his arms in the air.

"I think you just saved the season," Arlow said as he pounded her on the back, the rest of the team coming to join them.

"Lucky," Andi said.

Arlow grinned. "Like I told the guy," he said. "Still counts."

Merion killed the final four minutes, mostly playing keep-away when it got the ball. There was no need to attack, so they just kept the ball moving—backward as much as forward—to whomever was open.

When the clock hit zero, the teams wearily congratulated one another, covered in mud, shivering, but very happy—and relieved.

When Andi got to the goalie in the handshake line, she patted him on the shoulder and said, "You're right. I was lucky."

The goalie shook his head. "Like your buddy said, still counts," he said, and gave her a pat in return.

Andi giggled at the comment. Ron Arlow her "buddy"? Who'd have thunk it?

What's more, they were now going to play for the conference title on Friday. Who'd have thunk that?

38

HAL JOHNSTON WAS SITTING IN TRAFFIC ON THE EXPRESS-way heading to school on Wednesday morning when his phone rang.

It was a number he didn't recognize, but it had a 610 area code—meaning it was someone calling from the Philadelphia suburbs—so he decided to take a chance and answer.

"Hello?" he said cautiously.

"Hal, Hal Johnston?" a voice said.

"Yes," Hal said, still thinking it might be a sales-man of some kind.

"Hal, it's Tom Nussbaum. I'm your counterpart at King of Prussia–North. Well, sort of your counter-part. I coach the *boys'* soccer team."

Something in the way Nussbaum said *boys* put Hal on edge.

"Tom, what can I do for you?" he said, trying to keep his voice friendly.

"Actually, it's something I can do for you," Nussbaum said. "I think we both want Friday's game to be hard-fought, clean and fair, and may the best team win."

Something inside Hal told him this conversation wasn't going to go well.

"Of course," he said. "I would think that's a given."

"As far as I'm concerned it is," Nussbaum said. "But there's a potential problem, and I want to see if the grown-ups can work it out before something bad happens."

"Problem?"

"The girl," Nussbaum said.

He'd been right. "What about the girl?" Hal said, aware of the fact that his voice was rising.

"I'm like you, Hal, I think boys should play on teams with boys and girls should play on teams with girls."

It was at that moment that it occurred to Hal Johnston that he really didn't feel that way anymore.

As much as it pained him to admit it—even to himself. Andi Carillo had proven herself as a player and a teammate, and could clearly compete with the boys in the league. Nussbaum's comment suddenly felt wrong.

He decided not to voice his opinion . . . yet.

"And?" he said.

"My guys have had to play against girls three times already this season. Fortunately, I've been able to rein them in enough that no one's gotten hurt—though there have been a couple of close calls."

"Because you've reined them in," Hal said skeptically.

"Yes," Nussbaum said. "I told them they didn't need to cut the girls any breaks, but I didn't want any dirty play."

"Uh-huh. So what's this got to do with Friday?"

"We both know what's at stake," Nussbaum answered. "Winner gets to play for the league championship. Loser gets to go home. I'm not honestly sure I can promise nothing will happen to your girl . . ."

"Her name's Andi, Andi Carillo," Hal broke in, feeling some anger rising in his neck as he pulled off the exit ramp onto Route 1. "Coach, are you threatening me? Or my player?"

Nussbaum laughed humorlessly. "Threatening you? Come on, Hal, get serious. I'm going to threaten an eleven-year-old girl?"

"That's what it sounded like to me."

"Absolutely not. I pledge to you I'll do everything I can—as I said earlier—to make sure my boys play a clean game. But you may have heard the old saying about boys being boys . . ."

"Let me tell you something, Nussbaum, if any of your players steps out of line with Andi, I'll come after you long before the referee does anything."

"Goodness, your tune has changed since September, hasn't it, Hal? I'll do what I can. That's the best I can do."

He hung up, leaving Hal spluttering at the phone. The guy had threatened one of his players.

He also realized the coach sounded a lot like he himself had sounded just a few weeks earlier. He was embarrassed.

He wheeled into the school parking lot and went straight up the stairs to the principal's office. He needed the support and advice of Arthur L. Block.

* * *

Four hours later, Mr. Block and Hal Johnston sat
in Mr. Block's office with Andi Carillo and her
parents.

After the coach had told the principal about
his conversation with Coach Nussbaum, they had
decided to ask Andi's parents to come to school
during lunch hour to discuss the situation. Hal
Johnston knew Andi wouldn't want her parents
called in, but they really had no choice.

The coach was 99 percent convinced that neither the parents nor their child would be willing
to even consider her not playing in the game. But
he agreed when Block said, "Regardless, we have
to make them aware of this and decide if there's
action to take prior to the game."

Once Coach J had repeated what Nussbaum had
said, Andi spoke—waving off her dad, who clearly
wanted to respond.

"Hang on, Dad," she said. "I know exactly what
you want to say. Coach, we appreciate your concern. I was warned about this after last Friday's
game by . . ."

"Carrie O'Shea," her father said, filling in the blank for his daughter.

"Right," Andi continued. "She said she'd been treated very roughly on several occasions during her team's game with King of Prussia and had also been subjected to all sorts of rude, sexist comments."

"Andi, how do you feel about playing against these guys?" Coach Johnston asked—though he knew the answer.

"I can't wait," Andi said, eyes narrowing.

"That's what I thought," he said. "Question then is how do we proceed from here?"

"Well, the first thing I'm going to do is call my counterpart at KP–North," Mr. Block said. "He's new, and I'm guessing he knows little or nothing about this. Maybe he can have a talk with the coach."

"Someone needs to apparently," Andi's mother said. "It almost sounds like the coach has put a bounty on Andi's head. That can't be tolerated."

"We could go to the media, too," Coach J said. "They're already aware of Andi's story." He smiled, briefly, recognizing the irony of the comment. The media had been brought into the story because of his refusal to allow her to play on the team.

Andi was nodding as he spoke. "Jeff told me last night that his dad and Mr. Didinger and Mr. Barkann all talked about covering the game if we were playing for the championship," she said.

"Is it possible we can get them to do something before the game?" Mr. Block said.

Andi's dad was shaking his head. "I'm not a media expert, but I suspect, unless the KP–North coach actually admits on camera that he threatened Andi, there's no way realistically to report the story."

"What if I went on camera and said it?" Coach J suggested.

"There could be libel issues," Andi's mom said. "For them and for you. It's dicey at best."

Andi was confused by her mom's comment. If what Coach Johnston said was true, how could it be libel? She knew that libel was saying something untrue about someone.

Her dad read her mind. "It would come down to Coach Johnston's word against the other coach's word," he said, looking at her. "Since Tom Michaels has a son playing on our team and works with Ray Didinger and Michael Barkann, they could claim bias."

Mr. Block stood up. "For now, I'll call Keith Buckman at KP–North, and let's be sure the media is at the game Friday. At the very least, you would hope they'll think twice about doing anything with cameras rolling."

As they walked out, Coach J put an arm around Andi. "I'm truly sorry about this," he said. "You don't deserve any of this. I started all this in September, and you hung right in there through it all. I just want to say, I'm proud to have coached you."

Looking at him, Andi could tell he was sincere. "Thanks, Coach," she said. "That means a lot to me."

Which it did.

39

ONCE ANDI LET JEFF KNOW ABOUT THE MEETING WITH
Mr. Block, there wasn't any doubt in his mind that
his dad and his friends would be at the game on
Friday.

In fact, his father decided to let everyone he knew
in the media know about the story. "The more the
merrier in a case like this," he said. "If the King of
Prussia coach sees the place overrun by media, he'll
have to tell his players to back off and play clean."

"We hope," Jeff said.

His dad nodded. "We hope," he repeated.

While his father was contacting others in the
media, Jeff texted Andi and suggested she let Stevie

Thomas know what was going on. His dad had told him Mike Vaccaro had said he was going to come down from New York. Bringing media from New York and Washington into the picture in addition to the locals couldn't hurt.

Andi told Jeff that Coach J wasn't going to say anything to the team because he was still hoping that Mr. Block's phone call to the King of Prussia principal and the sight of a bevy of media might force the coach to back off.

When she called him on Thursday night to tell her that Stevie Thomas was coming and to find out what local media might be there, he asked her if Mr. Block had reported back on his talk with the KP–North principal.

"He spoke to my mom," she said. "He wasn't very encouraging. He said the guy claimed this was the first he had heard about his coach or any of his players going after any girl on an opposing team."

"What happened when Mr. Block told him about the phone call?" Jeff asked.

"He said he would check into it and get back to him if he thought there was any reason to worry or for him to take action."

"Doesn't sound like he was too upset, does it?"

"No, it doesn't," she said. "I'm not worried, though. I can take care of myself out there."

If she was trying to sound brave—it was working. Jeff could hear steel in her voice.

Friday was a glorious fall day. By the time school let out, the temperature was in the low sixties with just a hint of a breeze. The leaves on the trees surrounding the soccer field were turning fall colors, and there was a large crowd on hand for a sixth-grade soccer game. It looked as if most of Merion Middle had turned out. The seventh-and-eighth-grade team didn't play until Saturday morning, so the team was there in force to lead cheers. There were also a lot of people who had come down from King of Prussia.

Not to mention the media turnout. Jeff counted at least four camera crews, plus a number of reporters he remembered from September.

Andi had told him that Mr. Block—who was also on hand—had told her parents he'd never heard back from the principal at KP–North. *So be it*, Jeff thought. He just wanted the game to start.

It was impossible not to notice the size of the

KP–North players. It wasn't so much their height as their bulk. Their style of play was simple—go straight at the opponent with the ball and dare the other team to stop them.

What they lacked was speed; that was where Merion had an advantage. On a number of occasions when it appeared KP–North had a numbers advantage, Merion players were able to peel back into the play and deflect passes or knock the ball away.

It was speed that gave Merion its first real scoring chance of the afternoon about twenty minutes into the first half.

Zack Roth made a sweet move on a KP–North midfielder and burst into the offensive zone with the ball. The KP defense was forced to come up to meet him, and he quickly shoveled a pretty pass to Andi on the left. She had room to maneuver.

Surprisingly, the defense was slow to get someone to her, and she dribbled into the penalty box with the ball on her foot and space to shoot. Jeff, trailing the play, thought for sure Merion was about to go ahead.

But instead of shooting, Andi tried to pass the

ball to Arlow—who was well covered. KP's defense broke the play up and one of the defenders kicked it back upfield to safety.

Jeff was baffled. Why hadn't Andi taken an open shot?

"Guess the girl's afraid to shoot, huh?" one of the KP defenders said as the ball headed upfield.

Andi was in earshot and reddened at the comment—but said nothing.

Late in the half, KP's striker, a kid named Ted Pratt, knocked down a corner kick, pushed Danny Diskin away from him, and fired the ball past Bobby Woodward to make it 1–0. Danny screamed for a foul, but the referee simply pointed at the net to indicate the goal was good.

In the final minute, Merion had another chance. This time it was Mike Craig who started the play. He made a stutter-step move on a KP midfielder and had open space. He blew into the offensive zone, and after looking at both Andi and Arlow, dropped a pass to Jeff, who was trailing him.

Then he set what was essentially a basketball screen on a KP defender, getting in between him and Jeff to allow Jeff to go by—which he did. As

Jeff reached the penalty area, a defender moved to stop him, which left Andi open on the left.

Jeff dished the ball to her, and the next thing he knew, he was on the ground, having been taken down hard by the defender right as he passed the ball. He rolled over, feeling pain in his ribs just in time to see one of KP's midfielders take down Andi from behind as she was about to shoot. She fell, too, and the ball rolled harmlessly to the goalie.

Jeff waited to hear a whistle. None was forthcoming. He heard Arlow screaming, "Are you blind, ref? They took down two of our guys in the penalty box."

Andi was on her feet, also pleading for a foul.

The referee walked over to Arlow and showed him a yellow card. "Clean tackles," he said. "Not another word if you want to stay in this game."

Jeff slowly got up, holding his ribs. He desperately wanted to say something but knew that was a bad idea. Andi came over.

"You okay?" she said.

"Got kicked in the ribs," he said. "I'll live. You?"

"Fine," she said. Then she smiled. "I took a little bit of a dive. I thought two of us down would force him to make a call. Guess I was wrong."

Seconds later, the halftime whistle blew. They walked slowly to the bench, Arlow still shaking his head about the no-calls.

Coach J had his hands on his hips standing in front of them. Jeff expected a tongue-lashing.

It never came.

"Look," Coach J said in a voice soft enough that Jeff had to lean forward to hear him. "I know they're big, and I know they play rough." He looked at Diskin. "Danny, most games that was a foul on their goal. Not in this game. Jeff, you should have been given a penalty kick, and Andi, you should have gotten an Oscar for your acting on that dive. We can't expect any help from the referee. But we can't back off. Make them hit you, and eventually we'll get the calls."

He looked directly at Jeff. "Are you okay, Jeff?" he asked.

"I'm fine," Jeff said. "I'm not hurt, Coach, I'm just angry."

"Good," Coach J said. "Stay that way. Andi, you're out the first five minutes. Take a deep breath. We've got thirty minutes left to win this thing."

* * *

As the teams took the field for the second half, Andi sat on the bench alone. Jeff was in the game, and the other guys not playing were all standing near the sideline. Someone sat down next to her just as play began.

It was Coach J. She turned to look at him.

"At least now I know you're human."

"What do you mean?" she asked.

"You were a little gun-shy when you had that open shot early," he said. "The defender who was trying to get at you probably outweighs you by fifty pounds—and he's mean. They're all mean. It's part of the reason why they're good."

"Coach . . ."

He put up a hand. "Look, I don't blame you even a little bit," he said. "I'd be gun-shy, too, and so would all your teammates. They're all playing a little bit scared and no one has specifically threatened them."

He put his hands on her shoulders. "If you don't want to go back in, just say so—I won't think even a little bit less of you if you do. But if you want to play, I need you to *play*. The other guys on this team take most of their cues on the field from you.

If they see you playing timid, they'll play timid and we have no chance. If they see you playing like . . . *you* . . . they'll follow your lead."

He was looking her right in the eye as he spoke. She looked right back at him.

"I'm ready, Coach," she said.

He smiled. "Soon as the clock gets down to twenty-five minutes, go in for Arlow. We'll get his five minutes out of the way and then we'll go after them. Sound okay to you?"

"Sounds great," she said, jumping to her feet. She remembered what Herb Brooks, the coach of the famous US Olympic hockey team that had stunned the Soviet Union in the 1980 Olympics, had said to his players: "You were born to be a player. You were meant to be here. This moment is yours."

40

ARLOW HAD JUST COME BACK INTO THE GAME WHEN Andi got her first real opportunity of the second half.

Jeff had taken a long goal kick from Woodward and pushed the ball into Merion's offensive end. He slid a pass forward to Arlow, who pushed the ball to his left to Andi just as a KP–North defender plowed into him. He went down, but there was no whistle. He jumped up, laughed at the KP defender, and kept moving.

The pass reached Andi with a defender directly in front of her. She faked as if to go to the middle, then went left and was by him—until he kicked his leg out and brought her down from behind. She didn't wait for a whistle, just rolled to her feet and, the ball still in front of her, kept going.

She heard the defender yelling, "Hey, I fouled her!" at the ref, but either he disagreed, or since she still had the ball, he had decided to let her play the advantage, since blowing the whistle would be to the defender's benefit.

Arlow was sprinting now, and he and Andi closed in on the remaining defender—the same guy Andi had backed down from in the first half—two-on-one. He ran straight at Andi, who held on to the ball until the last possible second.

Just as he plowed into her full speed, she slipped the ball to Arlow—who was now wide-open in front of the goalie. She never saw what happened next, because she was flat on her back, but the shouts she heard around her told her Arlow had scored.

She heard a whistle, and this time, the referee came running in to indicate first that Arlow had scored and then to wave a yellow card at the defender who had taken Andi down.

"That should be a red," Andi heard Mike Craig saying as she sat up.

The ref pointed a finger at Craig: "Another word and *you'll* get a red," he said.

Andi felt pain in her right shoulder as she stood up. Jeff came in to check on her.

"I'm fine," she said—glaring at him to make sure he didn't ask again.

It was 1–1, less than fifteen minutes to play.

Not surprisingly, KP–North began to play conservatively. All they needed was a tie to win the championship, so there was no reason for them to take any chances.

Arlow took a pass from Diskin, went right past the defender who had taken him down, and unleashed what looked like a sure goal. Somehow, the KP–North goalie got a hand on it and deflected it just over the net. Arlow's shoulders sagged.

Turning to run back upfield, he said to Andi: "Thought I had it."

"You will," she said. "Next time."

The clock showed under seven minutes. Zack Roth again found Andi with some clear space. She was dribbling the ball patiently, waiting for the defender on her side of the field—different guy than the one who had taken her down, but just as big—to make a move at her when she was piled into from behind. She did a face-plant and heard the whistle again.

The referee was running in with another yellow card in his hand. She was slowly pulling herself up, helped by Diskin and Jeff when, out of corner of her eye, she saw someone running full speed at the guy who had just taken her down.

It was Arlow.

He was screaming angrily as he pushed the guy down and began swinging at him. Everyone from Merion rushed in to pull him off the guy, but it was too late. The referee was standing there with a red card in his hand, waving it at Arlow.

"Did you see what he did?" Arlow screamed. "Are you blind? He was trying to hurt her."

The ref shook his head. "I gave him the yellow he deserved," he said. "You started a fight—that's an automatic red card."

Both coaches had come onto the field. Coach J was screaming at the referee. "You red-card a kid in *this game* for protecting a teammate?" he said. "Are you out of your mind?

"Watch yourself, Coach," the referee said. "Get your player off the field."

Under the rules, a player could not be subbed for

after being ejected. Merion would have to play the rest of the way with ten players.

"I'm proud of you, Ron," Andi heard Coach J say as he put an arm around Arlow and walked him off the field. "Enough is enough."

Coach C addressed the remaining ten players: "Come on, everyone, we've still got six minutes left. We only need one goal. I *know* you can do it."

He was looking right at Andi as he said it.

The KP–North players were standing in a circle around their coach, which created a brief delay. Andi ran over to where Jeff, Roth, and Craig were standing, hands on hips, all of them looking stunned.

"Hey, guys, remember the decoy play the Union ran a few weeks ago that we all saw replayed a hundred times?"

"You mean where the guy pretends to be hurt?" Jeff said.

She nodded. "Get me the ball and when one of their guys takes me down—which they will—I'll stay down. Don't worry, though, I won't be hurt."

She rubbed her shoulder for a moment, which did hurt.

"What if the ref calls a foul?" Jeff said.

"If he does, I'll jump up and put the ball back into play super fast," she said. "But I don't think he will."

"You're right," Craig said. "Unless one of them brings a gun out here and tries to shoot you, he's not calling anything."

"Even then he might claim that calling a foul is a violation of the guy's second-amendment rights," Roth said.

They all got a laugh out of that one—briefly.

The clock was closing in on two minutes when the chance finally came. Diskin sent a long kick down the middle to Jeff, who almost immediately slid the ball to Andi even though she was well covered.

Andi made a halfhearted fake on the midfielder running with her and then ran almost straight at him. Almost on cue he slid in the direction of the ball but took her legs out in the process. She went down. It was actually the closest thing to a clean tackle someone from KP had made all day.

As planned, Jeff was running right at the play shouting, "Yellow, yellow!" The referee was shaking his head and waving his hand to play on while Jeff and the kid who had taken Andi down were scrumming for the ball. Andi was getting up slowly.

Jeff finally controlled it and quickly kicked it to Roth in the middle of the field. Roth was the team's best ball handler because he was ambidextrous, just as effective with his left foot as his right. Andi was still only halfway up as play went on. Jeff ran toward the middle as if he was filling Andi's vacated spot—to the spot where Arlow normally would have been.

"Zack, to Mike, to Mike," he yelled pointing across the field to Craig, who was closing on the goal, well guarded on the right.

Roth juked to the right as if he wanted to pass it that way, then stopped suddenly, able to move the ball to his left easily. Andi had leaped to her feet a split second earlier and was now racing in the direction of the penalty box. No one had been paying attention to her, except the Merion coaches, who were screaming at the referee to stop play for their injured player.

Only now the injured player had miraculously recovered, and Roth, expecting her to be on his left, kicked the ball hard, a few yards ahead of her. She picked it up on the run and closed on the goal with no one from either team near her.

A look of panic suddenly crossed the KP–North

goalie's face as he realized he was on the far side of the goal from where Andi was closing. He tried to sprint across from the far post to the near post, but it was too late. From ten yards out, Andi slowed, drew her leg back, and drilled a laser into the back of the net.

The goalie dived, stretched out as far as he possibly could, but he wasn't close. He sprawled on the ground helplessly.

Andi's arms were in the air. So were Jeff's and Roth's and Craig's and everyone else's in blue and gold. The noise from the stands and their side of the field was almost deafening. Jeff didn't think it was possible for a crowd at a sixth-grade soccer game to be so loud.

Then, out of the corner of his eye, Jeff saw the KP–North defender who had knocked Andi down earlier running right at her—clearly not to congratulate her.

Running as hard and as fast as he possibly could, Jeff cut the kid off with a diving tackle before he could pile into Andi. He heard the whistle, and he felt the kid rolling over on top of him. He didn't care.

41

"HE *HAS* TO BE EJECTED! HE WENT AFTER MY PLAYER WHEN the ball wasn't even in play!"

The referee was almost laughing at the KP–North coach as he ranted. Jeff remembered Andi telling him the coach's name was Nussbaum.

It had taken several minutes for the ref and the coaches from both teams to separate Jeff from the player he'd tackled and to keep any other fights from breaking out. The clock operator, under orders from the ref, had reset the clock—which had run out during the melee—to one minute.

The players were now standing about five yards apart, facing one another. Several of the cameramen from the various media outlets had come onto the field while things were being sorted out. Jeff figured they were getting an even better story than they'd hoped for when the day began.

He saw his dad standing there, too, and gave him a thumbs-up to let him know he was okay. He knew he had a little bit of blood trickling from the side of his mouth where the KP–North kid had landed a punch, but at the moment he was feeling no pain at all.

"I'm not ejecting him, Coach," the ref was now saying. "Your kid went after a player after she scored for no reason other than the fact that she scored. That kid"—he pointed at Jeff—"is the hero in all this. You are lucky he tackled your guy, because he might have seriously hurt her and then you'd all be in a lot of trouble."

He turned to the kid Jeff had tackled, took out his red card, and pointed it at him. "You are gone," he said.

Then, before Nussbaum could say anything, he pointed a finger at the KP–North coach and said, "You're also lucky I put sixty seconds on the clock. Your team has one last chance to tie this game up.

And if I see any hint of a tackle that isn't one hundred percent clean, I'll just call it off. You want the minute or not?"

Nussbaum stuck his hands in his pockets and turned to his players. "Come on, boys, let's line up," he said.

The teams lined up for the kickoff. The ball was kicked backward to a KP–North defender who instantly launched a long pass in the direction of the KP–North striker who had scored so long ago. Three Merion players surrounded him. Danny Diskin came out with the ball and began running down the side of the field, dribbling it.

The KP–North kids chased him halfheartedly, but as they closed on him he turned and passed it backward to Roth, who quickly kicked it across the field to Jeff.

Gleefully, Jeff charged across midfield and then booted it to Craig, who moved in on the goal before turning and kicking the ball all the way across the field to Andi. She knocked it down with her right foot, glanced at the clock, switched to her left foot and stood there with a huge smile on her face. The ball was on her foot when the final whistle blew.

Game over. Season over. Merion had won 2–1 and had won the conference title. The entire team raced at Andi as soon as that last whistle sounded.

Before she knew it, Jeff, Craig, and Arlow were picking her up on their shoulders for a victory ride. She saw the cameras surrounding them and felt slightly embarrassed. But only slightly.

When they put her down, Coach J and Coach C were standing there, beaming. They both hugged Andi, and then Coach J said, "Handshake line, now—and no one starts a fight."

"Really, Coach?" Arlow said. "Maybe just one?" But he was smiling, clearly not serious. There was no need to fight. They'd won their battle.

The vanquished KP–North players stood, heads down, waiting to shake hands. Coach J and Coach C, who were always at the back of the line, told Andi to go last among the players.

"Just in case," Coach J said.

Andi understood.

But the handshake line was without incident. Most of the KP–North boys couldn't—or wouldn't— look her in the eye. The goalie did.

"That was a great shot," he said. "You guys deserved to win."

That was it. The guys who had taken her down during the game looked straight at the ground. She thought of a quote her mother had framed on a wall in her office from President John F. Kennedy: "Victory has a thousand fathers," it said. "Defeat is an orphan."

Apparently most of the KP–North players felt like orphans. *Good*, she thought.

So, too, did Coach Nussbaum. Andi could hear him when he and Coach J shook hands.

"I'll always know," he said, "that my boys were better than your boys."

Andi glanced back and saw Coach J smile. "And I'll always know that my team was better than your team."

The two men glared at each other for a moment. Andi was tempted to turn around and say something. Then she stopped. There was no need to say anything. She had already had the last word.

Jeff knew there was now one more game to play, the next Friday, against the champions from South Philadelphia. He really didn't care all that much about that game. They had won the conference and they'd done it by beating a team that played dirty.

Normally in the handshake line he always said "Nice game" to the players on the other team. This time he said nothing, except to the guy who had gone toward Andi after the winning goal. He held on to his hand for an extra second, forcing him to look him in the eye.

"If you have any pride at all," he said, "you need to apologize to her."

"Heck with you." The kid shook off Jeff's grip and snarled at him—pretty much the reaction Jeff had been expecting.

The KP–North players didn't linger. Jeff noticed they went not to the locker room but straight to their bus. *Good riddance*, he thought.

None of them stopped to talk to the media that was swarming the field. Steve Bucci from Channel Three wanted to talk to Jeff because Andi and Craig had told him that he was the key to making the decoy play work. He saw Ray Didinger and his dad talking to Coach J.

"I figured it was worth a try," Jeff said. "We had to score, and Ron Arlow was out of the game. Andi was our best chance."

Much to his surprise, Ron Arlow walked over and, without saying a word, gave him a hug. "I'm glad we won," he said. "I'm gladder Andi scored the winning goal."

"Maybe she's even better than you?" Jeff said with a grin.

"Maybe," Arlow said, returning the smile. "Definitely better-looking, though, that's for sure." He paused. "You turned into a pretty good player yourself, Michaels. Learned a lot from you this fall."

Danny Diskin walked up as the two of them were talking. "Guess we've got a hectic day next Friday," he said. "Game in the afternoon, dance that night."

"Speaking of which," Arlow said. "I need to find a date."

"Don't you *dare* ask Andi," Jeff said.

Arlow smiled. "Already did," he said. Jeff's heart sank for an instant. "She turned me down. You won't believe who she is going with."

Diskin shoved Jeff. "You didn't ask her?" he said. "What are you, nuts?"

Jeff was stunned. He looked around for Andi. She was still surrounded by the media. Cameras were everywhere. Stevie Thomas, who he recognized after having googled him, was there quietly listening. So was Mike Vaccaro. She was clearly going to be a bit of an eleven-year-old celebrity after this.

"I need to talk to her," he said. "Soon as she's done."

"Not holding my breath," Diskin said. He and Arlow laughed and went to find their parents.

Jeff knew his mom was stuck at work and his dad was still interviewing people. There was nothing for him to do but wait.

Finally Andi finished her last interview and saw Jeff standing there. She came over. "I guess we did it, benchwarmer," she said.

He was stumped for an answer.

Finally, he found his voice.

"You know, Andi, next Friday . . ."

"I know," she said. "We have the game in the afternoon and then the dance. It's gonna be nuts!" She giggled. "Do you know that Ron asked me to go?" she said.

"I know," he said. "He said you were already going with someone."

"Yeah, Mike Craig asked me, too."

Jeff's heart sank.

"So you're going with Mike?" he said.

She put her hands on her hips and looked at him as if he were too stupid to live.

Then she gave him her dazzling smile.

"I said no to him, too," she said. "I told Arlow I was going with you. Right?"

For a split second Jeff didn't understand. Then he did. "Wait, what? You mean . . ." He paused, trying to find the words. "I mean, heck yes."

She was still smiling. "But first we have one more game to win," she said, and gave him a huge hug and a kiss on the cheek.

At that moment, the league championship game Friday meant nothing to Jeff. He had never felt so tall—or so happy—in his entire life.

AUG 2 0 2019